HER SAVAGE
His Heart

In Love With A Miami Bully

A NOVEL BY

SUNNY GIOVANNI

© 2017

Published by Royalty Publishing House

www.royaltypublishinghouse.com

"For the Gio Junkies..."

SOUNDTRACK

*"Associates"— **Slim Thug, J-Dawg & Z-Ro***

*"Hate that I Love You" – **Rihanna & Ne-Yo***

*"Trust" – **Justin Bieber***

*"Acquainted" – **The Weeknd***

*"Mine" – **Beyonce & Drake***

*"Blood on the Leave" – **Kanye West***

*"Kissin' on My Tattoos" – **August Alsina***

*"Worst Behavior"— **Drake***

*"Deep" – **Big Sean & Lil' Wayne***

*"Burial" – **Pusha T, Moody Good & TrollPhace (Skrillex Remix)***

*"Pretty Wicked Things" – **Dawn Richards***

*"Feel Me" – **Mecca Kalani***

*"Bitch Better Have My Money" – **Rihanna***

FORESIGHT

All the world's a stage. The men and women are merely players. All the hood's a show. The men and women are simply hustlers. There is a war brewing. Not just any war. A never-ending war for peace, and most definitely for the throne. Whose throne? We may never know. Blinded by greed, it's hard to see that there are multiple thrones belonging to kings and queens of the streets. The princes and princesses starve for the affection and approval from the hierarchy. The jesters put on their dances and acts. Maybe for entertainment. Maybe to keep the dominant royals distracted from an ambush or revolt. When the people starve, or are being mistreated, they rise up. That's only when the first drop of blood by a do-gooder is spilled. Let that crimson not hit the pavement, for the workers and civilians will storm the castle. But whose castle? The knights shall be called in for reinforcement, yet there are only so many. Even they disband when the hierarchy is not quick-witted. Now they want their dues from constantly going to war for the royals. Being at the top is hard. You don't know who to trust, who to get rid of, or who is going to be your heir in case everything falls apart.

In this case, the kingpin of Miami and his foot-soldiers should be very careful because there is a black mamba in the house of the king. He alone has the power to either keep the king afloat, or start this revolution off with one simple mistake. The streets are his kingdom. The walls are about to come crashing down.

CHAPTER ONE

Meet the Flockas

A nightclub in downtown Miami was full of life and noise. People crowded around the entrance so that they could get into the hot spot. However, with the way the enormous bouncer at the front door was feeling at the moment, if he didn't know you, you weren't getting in. With their own little conversations and peepers set on other things, almost no one noticed the all-black Mercedes as it crept around the corner and stopped on the slick street directly in front of the bouncer. The first to get out was a six-foot-four, slender built, young man wearing a black, leather jacket with a white V-neck t-shirt underneath. Atop it were three gold chains that dangled from left and right. Our dear prince wouldn't be touched within the crowd of gatherers. Of course he wouldn't be, whether it was because of the three other young ones on either side or behind him.

There was Legend, who was the pistol-packing Dominican who would fly off in a rage and mix Spanish in with his English. Then, standing on the other side was Calmly. Despite his name, he had a temper that he wore on his sleeve. His grey eyes almost seemed lifeless.

They told you that he wasn't to be fucked with. The high yellow man looked as though he had no soul. Finally, standing behind the bunch, was the biggest threat of all. Scrappy. His name spoke for itself. He was quiet, yet it was only because he would rather his fists speak for him. The dark-skinned, young man always wore some sort of hood over his long, crinkly dreadlocks that sometimes hung in front of his face. The Haitian oddly had dark blue eyes that were a complete contrast from what most people thought that a man of his skin tone should've had. With his reputation, most wouldn't stop to ask him where in his bloodline he had earned eyes as glassy as his.

Leading, out front as usual, was the one and only Bandz. He was the baby brother to the baller and street king known as Dolla. With the relation alone, Bandz was invincible. However, he moved through the streets, and on this particular night, the club, without anyone darting their eyes at him out of fear of what Dolla or Bandz's boys could and would do to them. The crew located the stairs to the club and went up to the main office where they would find the owner. The old Cuban man hadn't made any payments on his property, where Dolla had squeezed money out of him. The clique known as the Flockas were there to regulate. They were like Dolla's little hounds. Whereas three out of the four only did it for the money and out of loyalty, Bandz was only showboating for his big brother's approval. He should have known that it would be a bad thing to go in without thinking, yet he didn't stop and ask himself if barging into someone's office during business hours was a good idea.

Legend was the first to burst through the glass door with his golden-brown face set on the expressions of anger and disgust. His head whirled around to Bandz with a raised brow, then back to the Cuban sitting behind his desk. His long, wavy ponytail almost slapped him in the face when doing so. "Look what the fuck I found, Bandz," he said with a chuckle. "Tarde en alquiler, ¿no?"

"Late on rent?" the Cuban repeated him as he stood. "Joven, nunca llegué tarde. So, you tell Dolla to come and see me like a man. My business is not a daycare for you little boys to come to when your parents are out fucking half of Miami. ¿Comprender?"

"*Parents?* Okay." He, along with Calmly, pulled out their pistols and aimed them both directly at the owner.

The rotund man slowly took off his designer straw hat and set it on his desktop. Then, he stood as he removed his cigar from the corner of his lips. "You must be crazy to pull your guns on me. With me dead, how in the hell are you going to get your money? And you, Bandz. I know about you stealing money from Dolla. He didn't raise my rates by ten percent. You're pocketing that shit. It would break del hermano heart if he knew that you were stealing from him."

"No, it wouldn't," Bandz spoke. With the quickness, he pulled his own piece and fired off a round, piercing the man in the chest. He sniffled, taking the back of his hand across the under part of his nose to get rid of mucus that he thought was running. "My motherfuckin' allergies are killin' me. Let's get this money and get out of here before Dolla starts callin' and buggin' me."

"Yo," Scrappy said behind him. "The fuck was he talkin' about, Bandz? You fuckin' Dolla over?"

"Nah," he lied as he inspected his fresh manicure. "He was just trying to blackmail me. No, his grandson runs his company with him gone, and my brother knows that he's just a little weasel. Unlike Pablo over here, Dolla will be able to squeeze out fifty percent instead of forty. I just did him a fuckin' favor."

Scrappy narrowed his eyes, questioning the truth of what he had said. Still, he helped to clear out the safe, packing up as many bills as he could inside of duffles that were already there.

———————————

Dolla, at thirty-two years old, had acquired much in his younger years. He was finally able to live comfortably without touching anything. Even though he hadn't had to work, he still believed that a real boss had his hands inside everything he had going on. His girl, Mocha as they called her, would make fun of him and call him a workaholic. They were jokes, but they were very much true. Since he was twelve years old, Dolla had spent the majority of his days working and most of his nights and early mornings counting his money and plotting on a new hustle. Having to look over his little brother for the past six years wasn't easy. Bandz might've thought that his brother was blind to him, but Dolla didn't survive in a cut-throat world by shutting his eyes and praying for better.

As though he was content, Dolla leaned his tall and heavy statue over his all-white pool table. It might've only looked like he was playing a game all by himself, but he was thinking. Plotting. Placing events together long before they happened. The alarm system disturbed these thoughts when it alerted him that the front doors had opened. Even then, he kept shooting pool.

"Still, you didn't have to shoot him," he heard Scrappy complain.

He knew that what Scrappy had said must've been important because he watched Scrappy grow up from the age of sixteen, and now he was still quiet at twenty-two. For him to speak, it sent up a red flag to Dolla.

He stood tall and squeezed the black cue in his hands. With his pecks pushing at his black muscle shirt from how hard he was squeezing the wooden stick, Bandz would know that he was in trouble when he rounded the corner from the living room and saw his big brother standing there with his feet at shoulder's width.

Bandz stopped in his tracks when seeing the man that he didn't think was awake at three in the morning.

Dolla tilted his bald head with an unreadable expression on his chocolate face. "And who the fuck did you shoot, and you had better not say Pablo."

"Well—"

"Why must you cause me problems, Bandz?"

Though Dolla spoke ever so calmly, Bandz had to take his dazzling, brown eyes to the floor-to-ceiling portrait behind his brother; it was a dollar bill with his brother's face in place of George Washington.

"Speak, nigga!" Dolla bellowed.

Bandz lifted his chin in the air. "He wasn't gonna budge," he explained. "With him out of the way, his grandson is meek. It's an easy extra ten percent in your pockets. That's all I'm sayin'."

"Oh, that's *all* you're saying, little brother?" Dolla shrugged as he went back to his pool table and positioned himself to take the shot that he was about to before his system disturbed him. "Okay. I like your enthusiasm, but I *hate* the way you think. See, you *don't* think, Bandz. You shot a man over ten-fucking-percent when you could've convinced his grandson to open up another spot with us as investors, just to get another thirty-percent out of him, under a contract that says that we can sell our ecstasy there. But that ain't what you did. Now this little motherfucker is gonna be stretched too thin. You know what that means?" Finally, Dolla took his shot.

The crack of the balls made Bandz flinch. He closed his eyes tight and took a deep breath as he reopened them.

"*That*, Bandz, means that he ain't gonna be able to keep up with his money. Not being able to run two clubs and keep up with the money is gonna stress his home life. Stressing the home life, plus no money, equals no wife. All of that combined equals this little scary motherfucker killing himself. After that, we gotta scout somebody else to squeeze, which is unnecessary time consumed when we already had a motherfucker under our thumb to leach off of!"

"Dolla—"

"See, you don't fuckin' get it, boy." He leisurely approached his little brother with his cue resting on his shoulder. "You got to think, be careful, and still hold your fuckin' power. Are you still in training, Bandz? Because I think I cut the length of your leash four years ago. Nah, I didn't think that you would run out there and start bustin' at my fuckin' money makers. Nah, I didn't think that you would cost me money. So, you know what you're going to do for your big brother?" Dolla tugged at Bandz's jacket as if he was trying to close it with one hand. "You're going to make my money back. That's damn near twenty racks that you owe me. Oh, and you're going to make it back." Suddenly, as if the cue was a baseball bat, he whacked his brother with it across the arm. He didn't stop hitting him, even when Bandz went rolling around on the floor and was bleeding out of his mouth with how hard Dolla whacked him across the jaw.

At the front of the house, the front doors burst open. Scrappy looked up from the white, leather couch he was sitting on as though he could see who barged in just yet. Even Legend and Calmly stood from the couch across from him, with bills in their hands from the club, just in case someone was crazy enough to burst into the king's palace this early in the morning.

Charging through the foyer in a pair of eight-inch platform, thigh-high leather boots was Mocha. Dragging behind her was the tail of her full-length Stone Marten, sable fur coat. Obviously, she was on a mission. Legend and Calmly sat back down and hurriedly took their eyes back to their money to make sure the sum of it was correct before they presented it to Dolla.

Mocha's gorgeous face was tight as hell as her hazel eyes threw daggers around the corner she was about to turn to get to her boyfriend of seven years.

Dolla was done with his brother by the time his woman curved the corner with flaring nostrils. The first thing he locked onto were her mocha colored thighs that extended from her short shorts and stopped at the top of her boots. When he looked past her tiny, visible waist from atop her shorts and her large bosom that she paid for with her own money, he could see that his black beauty was not at all happy. He ran his tongue over his thick lips as thoughts of him pinning her against the wall had gone through his mind.

"Bandz," she managed through caged teeth, but her eyes were aimed up at Dolla's. "Get out."

Holding his jaw, he shook his head and obliged. His mind was on the fact that his brother would get his one day. Bandz couldn't stand being at the bottom of the totem pole and not ever being good enough in his brother's eyes. He was set on doing whatever it took to escape Dolla's shadow and paying him back for always putting him down.

Once Bandz was out of earshot, Mocha stomped over to Dolla to close the space between them and folded her arms under her breasts.

"Fuck you chargin' in here for?" he asked her.

"I'm gonna ask you one time, and one time only, Dolla. Who the fuck is Tiffany?"

"A bitch that sucked me up that stands out on Fifth Street. Why?"

"Oh, and you're willing to admit this to me?"

"She's a prostitute." He shrugged. "What else am I supposed to do with a prostitute? Wife the hoe?"

"Fuck you, Dolla!" she screamed, taking a step away. "You out here got me lookin' fuckin' stupid!"

He grabbed her jaws tightly to bring her closer. "Watch your mouth, Mocha Latte," he sang lowly as if the young woman wasn't at all angry. "Wasn't you out there fuckin' another nigga? Hmm?"

"You know damn well I wasn't fuckin' nobody else," she snarled. Unlike everyone else, Mocha wasn't at all afraid of Dolla. She loved him and sometimes respected him, but not a day in their relationship was she scared to speak her mind or reprimand him. "Don't try to turn this around on me, when you make sure I'm faithful, but you can go out there and get your dick wet. I'm not stupid. Don't treat me like it." She pulled her face out of his hand and left the small area that her boyfriend had long turned into a billiard.

"Mocha!" he called after her. When she hadn't returned an answer, he threw his cue onto the table and marched down the hall to find her.

She was stomping up the curved white, stairs by the time he made it to the end of the hall. "Fuck you," she said under her breath.

He couldn't stop her until he reached his master's suite, where she was taking off her fur coat. "What's wrong with you?" he harshly asked as he slammed the double doors behind him. "I know damn well you didn't just come over here to check me over no bitch. It's somethin' else. Tell me."

"Why does it even matter, Dolla?" She fingered her platinum blonde rosy curls behind her ear. It was a dead giveaway when she didn't look at him while she was talking to him. "You're out here fuckin' hoes, and that's what's on the table right now."

"No, it ain't. Mocha, look at Daddy. Tell me what the fuck got you so hype before you fuck around and get slapped in the mouth."

She sucked her teeth. "Ms. Prissy is comin' home," she confessed.

"Who?" His face contorted.

"The lil' bitch that my mama put in the all-girl's school and had us out here workin' for her tuition and shit? She's done with college now, so she's comin' home for a break."

"And that's what got your ass talkin' out the side of your neck on me? Because your little sister did somethin' with her life and you didn't?"

Mocha frowned at him, then snatched her coat off the bed. Reluctantly, Dolla caught her arms before she could walk off.

"Don't trip on it, baby," he said softly. "She can't be no worse than Bandz's little ass. You need to be grateful that all you did was send off money. Be lucky that you didn't have to house her, clothe her, feed her, and damn sure be happy that she doesn't disappoint you. She's finished with college, so that means that you played a part in making her who she is. I failed. Just look at Bandz. You know damn well that I would never admit to failure, but I don't know what I did wrong when raising this fool. Stop stressin' so damn much, alright?"

"It's not fair," she complained. Mocha stomped her foot and collapsed within his massive arms. "She got all the perks while I had to roll around in dirt to make sure that she had luxury, Dolla."

"You got luxury here. I don't know why you don't see that shit. Girl, the first time you ever drove a Benz was because I gave you one. But you know what you did? You gave that bitch right back to me until you were able to buy it from me with your own money. That's because you're a hustla. Ain't nobody gave you shit. That's somethin' to be proud of. Now… come and let me adjust your damn attitude."

As Dolla led her over to the bed, Mocha had a full-blown smile on. Inside, she was still fuming that her baby sister was the one who was chosen for greater things, whereas she had to lay on her back for what she had acquired. A spoiled, hood princess and major hustler like Mocha couldn't respect that.

CHAPTER TWO

Welcome To The Kingdom

After a four-hour flight, Kalie was more than exhausted. She marched through the airport with her rolling luggage in tow. She just knew that her mother would be proud when she saw her. The last time she saw her was at her college graduation when both of her sisters were also present to cheer her on. The only person that didn't seem too happy for her was her big sister Michelle, who went by the name of Mocha. Kalie didn't care. She was proud of herself. The reason she was returning home was not for the approval of Michelle, but to see her family before she opened her own private practice as a psychiatrist. Since she was ten, her mother thought that it would be best to get her sweet girl out of Hell's Den, as she called it, and give her something that she hadn't given to either of her other daughters. She wanted Kalie to have a future in a solid field. By no means did Queenie, the madam, want her past failures to repeat by having her youngest to learn the ropes of the business and go into it like everyone else. She was determined to break the cycle.

A woman stood in Kalie's path at the passenger loading dock. She was shapely with her white hair cut into a short bob that most classic Hollywood actresses wore. In a black pinstriped suit, Queenie looked like a woman of power and status. She wasn't wearing her infamous shades on this day. Instead, she donned her clear designer specs. Just before lighting a cigarette, she pushed them up on the bridge of her nose, then dusted falling ashes off of her exposed bosom that peeked from the trim of the plunging neckline from the jacket.

"Mommy?" Kalie called with a hybrid of a smile and frown on her face.

Queenie looked up at her child, yet she didn't smile. She thumped her cigarette and strutted to her in her six-inch, skinny heeled pumps. Sandwiching Kalie's arms between her palms she gave her a kiss on the cheek, then stood back to examine her daughter's slim-thick figure. "Having you up North done gone and got you all kinds of slim," she said lowly. "But that's alright. We're gonna get you a little thicker." Finally, Queenie smiled. "My baby girl is finally home."

Kalie accepted her mother's embrace, taking in the sweet scent of Queenie's perfume. She couldn't believe it. She was finally home after twelve years. On her breaks, Queenie and Sheena, her middle sister, would rent a home and come up to Philadelphia to visit, but Kalie hadn't stepped foot on southern soil since she had arrived at that very same airport to leave.

———————————

Queenie gabbed the whole ride to the house that Kalie hadn't seen. She knew that shortly after she left, her family moved, but the only part of the home that she bore witness to was the background

14

of her mother's home office during video calls. Arriving at the three-story mansion was something to see. Kalie gasped when she stepped out of the car. The young woman who served as the driver grabbed her luggage out of the truck and headed up to the massive, wooden double doors.

Queenie hooked arms with her daughter as she lit yet another cigarette. "Welcome home, my baby," she said as she blew her smoke. "I have a room for you that's all decked out in what I think you would like. You sleep on the third floor, alright? Don't waste your time with the stairs. We got an elevator for that. Either you can take the one from the kitchen, near the stairs, or at the back of the house. We have bitches who cook, so just tell them what you want to eat and they'll get on it for you. You want to go shopping? I got a bitch who will escort you for that, too."

"Mommy, can you not call them bitches?" Kalie innocently asked.

Queenie stopped shy of the porch and turned to face her daughter with a straight face. "This is your nature, Kalie Antoinette. You should get used to it. Just because you'll be here for a spell doesn't mean that I'm going to change how I speak, live, or move. Understand your Mommy, honey. I am the head bitch in charge. I am the motherfuckin' Queen of Miami. That means that I do what I want, when I want, and I don't give a fuck who has special thoughts about it. That includes my precious baby." Queenie playfully pinched her cheek with a smile. "Thank you for your input, though. Now let's get in here. I know that you must be tired after your travels. Your bath should be ready for you. If it's not, just pick up the phone in your bedroom and tell whomever that answers that my baby needs her goddamn water drawn."

"Yes, Mommy," Kalie answered halfheartedly.

As soon as the pair entered, inside the massive foyer was a group of women who stood there with smiles beaming brightly for Kalie. To her, they all looked like runway models and video vixens. There had to be at least ten of them. They were all dressed with such class and elegance. She gathered that her mother had to make at least five grand a night off of one of them.

"Welcome home," a brunette told her as she stepped forward. "I look forward to helping you expand your resume."

"My… my resume?" Kalie repeated with a contorted face.

The brunette looked to Queenie with fear in her pretty green eyes. She was afraid that she had spoken out of turn.

Queenie cleared her throat. Obviously, Mocha hadn't contacted her like she had told her to. "Your sister was supposed to call you to let you know that you'll be using the girls to counsel with them to help get some names under your belt for when you open your practice."

"Well," she nervously chuckled. "I didn't receive that call at all, actually. I truly thank you for that."

"Go on up to your room and get comfortable. You'll know which one is yours."

Kalie politely nodded and smiled at the girls as she passed them to head up the stairs. Despite wanting to test out the elevator that her mother had suggested, she went about it the old-fashioned way by using her legs.

"Where the fuck is Mocha?" she heard Queenie ask.

Kalie shook her head and continued her journey up both flights of stairs. After traveling what seemed like forever, she finally reached a door that had a large red ribbon across it. She smiled and entered her new bedroom. Inside it was a canopy bed, a king size, with powder pink drapes, a thick, white comforter, and a mountain of designer pillows. At the foot of the bed was a plush, pink couch of the same color as her drapes. Two tall-back chairs, white, sat adjacent to each other in the corner with two tall glass double doors on the other side of her bed that led to a terrace. She easily spotted her all-white wooden desk that had a big, leather, powder pink chair pushed up to it, and a white, wide computer monitor atop it. It was very clear that Queenie spared no expense at her daughter's comfort.

"Knock-knock!" Kalie heard a voice behind her. She sharply turned around to see the tall, Coke bottle frame of Sheena. Without a warning or a word, she took off and leaped onto her sister to squeeze her inside a hug. "Well, damn, girl. I missed you, too," Sheena said with a giggle. When Kalie let her go, she whipped the falling bangs of her mohawk away from her eyes and carefully inspected her sister. "Mama told me that you were going to be with us for a while. Sorry that whole roommate business didn't work out for you up in Philly. But what did you expect from a northerner? All they know is how to be stuck up and throw parties. I don't know why you didn't call home and tell us that you needed a place of your own."

"Because, Sheena, I wanted to do it on my own," she groaned.

"Yea, but you know what mama says. Sometimes you ain't got

to be strong all by yourself. So…" Sheena's hard heels clomped across the floor as she took in the finished product of the long nights she spent with arguing with her mother while pinning pages along a vision board. "You like your room?"

"Sissy, I love it!" she cheered. "How did you know that powder pink was my favorite?"

"How do you even know that it was me who did the room?"

Kalie rolled her eyes. "Because, crazy… mom's women do the footwork while she sits back and coaches. Besides, nobody under this roof knows me like you do. I'm just in shock that you knew what my favorite color was."

"If I knew you, then don't you think I knew what colors would appease you?"

"Point taken," she giggled.

Sheena took a seat in the tall-back chair in the corner, then crossed her legs. Afterward, she nodded to the terrace doors so that her sister could go and open them. From the handbag that hang from her wrist, Sheena pulled out a Black and Mild cigar, lit it, and then checked her phone for missed messages.

"What's with all the women?" Kalie asked as she hopped up on her bed to sit Indian style. "I didn't know that mama's stable had grown so much over the years."

"Actually, it doesn't grow at all. Mama only recruits girls with a certain GPA who have been turned away from their own homes. They get into college, they work their way through, and then when they graduate, it's bye-bye birdie. But, of course, after that, they invest in the business of housing the new recruits and keeping them fed. Mama's the same… she's just smarter. Only three lucky girls are chosen every year in this house. New ones come to replace them in the same status. Let's say a girl's GPA dropped in college and she doesn't pull it up in time, Mama finds her replacement and kicks the other girl out. She's very strict. They're more than scoundrels. They have class, taste, goals, and brains. Mama makes sure of that."

"That woman is smart."

"Very much so."

"How's Michelle?"

"Please." Sheena blew her smoke. "Don't ever call her by her government name, alright? She'll snap on you in a heartbeat. She prefers for you to call her Mocha."

"Why?"

"Her lil' boyfriend convinced her that he gave her that name because of her skin color, so she goes with it."

"But… Mama gave her that nickname… because of the color of her skin."

"Yea, we know." Sheena rolled her eyes as she took another puff of her cigar. "Anyway, you'll be coming out with me tonight. I got you a bathing suit, but from the looks of you, we'll have to take it in some."

"Why is it a big deal that I'm not as luscious as everyone else?"

"Because you look hungry, homegirl," Sheena joked. "But for real. We're going to the beach tonight. Dolla, who is Mocha's boyfriend, is having a bonfire party. Don't try to object either. You're grown, and you could use some drinks in your system. Besides, you might even get some cuddy tonight."

"Cuddy?"

"Dick, Kalie. You might get some dick."

"I think I like the word cuddy better," she said with a laugh.

CHAPTER THREE

Star-Crossed

*M*ocha fondly laid her head over onto Dolla's bicep as he drove. The only thing that mattered was the fact that she was being seen on his arm inside his white drop-top Maserati. As soon as he pulled into a parking space, she whipped her bangs out of her face and looked around at all of the old school tricked out cars on the lot to see who all had shown up for one of Dolla's random parties. Honestly, she would never live up to Queenie's name and have the respect that she had. All people knew her as was Dolla's main girl and as the daughter of one of Florida's elite.

Beside Dolla's car was a black Mercedes with sparkling rims. Bandz stepped out and stretched. Like most times during a hot summer day, he didn't care for a shirt. He was very sure that he wouldn't receive a citation for public indecency. It was absurd.

"Put some clothes on," Mocha sneered.

"Same to you," he returned, looking at her hips and thighs past the sheer, red wrap that she knotted at the waist.

"Bandz, don't make me slap you. Where are your little friends?"

He nodded at a sight over her shoulder where Scrappy had pulled onto the other side of Dolla's car in his square-body, glossy Caprice. The ragtop was down, and seated on the very back was Calmly being a show off. Scrappy sent a roar through his double muffler before he shut the engine off.

Legend hopped over the passenger side door with a thick, white towel around his neck. He too was shirtless, but only to show off the fighter pilot with blazing guns that he had tattooed atop his rippling abs. "What's happenin', fam?" he shouted with spread arms at Mocha.

She rolled her eyes and turned away from the group.

"This is a beach, Mocha Latte," Bandz joked. "We ain't supposed to have on clothes anyway."

"Boy, please. I shouldn't be seeing all of your business," she retorted.

He tilted his shades, leaning over just a tad to get a peek at her backside. "And *Lord…* I shouldn't be seeing none of yours."

"Don't play with me," she said lowly. "You ever open your mouth about that night—"

"I haven't, and shut up. My boys are coming."

"Why you gotta be so mean, mami?" Legend asked Mocha as he slapped hands with Bandz. "You're too beautiful to be so mean at times."

"Don't speak to me." Mocha turned on the heels of her Dior wedges, but what caught her line of sight made her want to scream.

"Damn," Bandz said under his breath. His brother was giving a kiss to a young lady's hand who Sheena had escorted. The girl had his jaws gathering saliva. He wanted to take a bite out of her toned thighs that were extending from the trim of her short denim shorts. The smile that broke out across her face from his brother's kiss had him captivated. He needed to know who she was, and he prayed that she wasn't a recruit for their family. "Who that is, Mocha?"

"Don't you even think about it!" she immediately reprimanded him. "That's my little sister. That means that I will whack your fuckin' balls off if you ever lay a hand on her."

"Damn, girl. I just want to know her name. How come I didn't know it was more of y'all?"

"Because it wasn't any of your damn business. That's why."

"Baby," Dolla happily sang with Kalie's fingers locked inside of his own. "I had the pleasure of meeting the youngest princess of the bunch," he proudly announced. "Beauty seriously runs in your family. Good Lord, I just want to know why your daddies left all of y'all behind. Let me know where to find them, and I will personally take care of them."

"Well, then you would have to ask them why they didn't submit to our mother," Kalie joked.

"Either way, it's good to finally have you home, little sister. We love you."

She then looked to Mocha, who had yet to greet her.

Mocha folded her arms underneath her bosom and rolled her eyes. "Yea. What he said."

Bandz caught himself from asking how come Dolla had never said something so kind about him before.

"Baby K, these are the Flockas," Dolla continued. "The Haitian down there on the end with the sleeveless hoodie on is Scrappy."

"Li bon al kontre ou." Kalie offered a smile when she said, "It's nice to meet you," in Haitian-Creole. She had a roommate her Freshman year in college, who taught her how to greet the girl's parents when they visited. Other than that, she had no idea what his reply would translate to, if any.

"Sak ap pase?" He gave her a nod as he asked her what was happening.

Dolla pointed to Legend next. "This crazy, Spanish motherfucker is Legend."

"How're you doin' beautiful?" He winked.

"That there is Calmly, but he's a bit of an anger management case gone bad. And finally, my little brother—"

"Bandz, sweetie," he introduced himself as he slowly removed his shades to kiss her flesh with his eyes. "Nice to meet you, Baby K."

Kalie awkwardly smiled at Bandz's sense of politeness. He had some work to do, though. He was nowhere near as suave as Dolla. It actually made Kalie uncomfortable.

Dolla cleared his throat. "If you will, Kalie." He then took her by the hand as she and Sheena followed. He cut his eyes at his brother over his shoulder. Everyone else filed out of the parking lot so that they could see why it was that Dolla was making a big deal of Kalie being home. Dolla trudged through the sand, forgetting that he was wearing an expensive pair of all-white Giuseppe sneakers.

The DJ, who was stationed on a small platform near the rocks, cut the music and handed Dolla a microphone when he was close enough. Dolla only let Kalie's hand go long enough to thump the mic.

"Can y'all hear me?" he asked the gatherers that were there specifically upon last-minute request. "Good. Now, baby girl is finally home and got herself a bad ass degree in Psychology. If this ain't Black excellence, then I don't know what is. Now, for all y'all depressed, confused, suicidal folks, or if you're grieving some kind of loss, this is the woman you need to go to. Run up to her and get her info as soon as you can. Give it up for Baby K Devieux!" Dolla held her hand up high, while the guests clapped and cheered for her.

Kalie was bashful. She covered her face with her free hand, then dropped it at her side. Afterward, she repeated the cycle twice more without being able to figure out how to accept Dolla's gratitude.

In the distance, Bandz's nostrils flared with anger. Beside him, Mocha was fuming. They both shared a twinge of jealousy. Neither of them had Dolla to do something so grand for them or flex his social skills for the purpose of giving them new clientele. Scrappy, however, closed his mouth from how long it had been open since hearing of Kalie's accomplishment. He was one of the people who needed her. He was desperately holding on to and concealing the fact that his baby's mother was withholding their daughter from him, upon accusations that he didn't have it all. He didn't care for her. He just wanted his baby girl. If Kalie could help, then his life would be complete.

Sheena had spread a blanket onto the now cold dirt and had been sitting on it with her plate of barbecue and fixings. Finally, her younger sister had come to sit beside her. She eyed her strangely. "Where the hell is your plate?"

Kalie shrugged while going through her phone. "Do you know how much sodium is in that stuff? And other than that, I don't eat meat."

"See, that's why your ass is so skinny." Sheena picked up a chicken leg and waved it at her sister. "What's that in your phone that has your attention so much?"

"Oh, just a few appointments that I'm setting up. Thanks to Dolla, I have all of next week booked. Now I have to set up a website soon. Word of mouth is going to get me only so far."

"What're you chargin' these folks?"

"A hundred dollars a session for up to three hours."

"That's cheap as fuck, K! What the fuck?"

"Look, I have to fund going back to graduate school some type of way. This is only for about a year where I can do this under the table to get cash, stash it, then go back to school so I can open my own office. It's only for the beginning. Everyone who comes on after them will have to pay double. And those after that bunch will be close to paying a hundred an hour." She gave her sister a wink before taking her attention back to her phone.

A smile slowly exploded onto Sheena's oval shaped face. "You little hustlin' bitch. I guess our mama is in you after all."

"I guess it is." The voice they heard was not at all Kalie's. They looked up into the dying sunlight to see Mocha there with her arms folded.

Kalie snarled. "Are you going to do anything other than frown at me? How about trying to give me a hug, Mocha?"

"I'd rather not. I done already carried you through elementary, junior high, high school, *and* college."

"Correction. My academic scholarships got me through college."

"Whatever. So you get my point in me not being obligated to hug your little ungrateful ass."

"Ungrateful?"

"Mocha, you need to calm down," Sheena stepped in. "You had a choice and you made it. Chill."

"No." Mocha worked her neck. "She has a right to know that it was us who laid on our backs to get her that fancy degree."

Before either of the sisters could offer a rebuttal, Dolla caught Mocha's arm and dragged her closer to the water. She yanked away from him while stumbling over her wedges to catch her balance.

"Fuck is your problem?" he harshly asked her. "I swear to God that when you talk to me, you had better keep your voice down or else we're going to be two scrappin' motherfuckers out here."

"What's *your* problem, Dolla? You throw a surprise homecoming for her, and you don't even know her. Where the fuck was my party when I did six months in the county jail for you, huh? Where was my surprise party for my birthday? This is what I mean by you having me look stupid!"

Dolla angrily grabbed her jaws, snatching her closer. "Do you not understand what a good business opportunity this is? Set her ass up in an office somewhere and reap the fuckin' benefits. I swear you should be fuckin' with my brother, because neither one of you motherfuckers *think.*"

She pulled her face away and took a sloppy step back with tears swelling in her eyes. "You… want to even get her an office, too?"

"Well, she has to go back to graduate school, first. It's just good business. Charge her for promotions—"

She didn't want to hear anymore. Mocha left Dolla standing there, running to the parking lot as her tears fell. How was it that Kalie had gotten everything that Mocha felt she deserved?

Her sisters watched from afar, wondering what Dolla could've said to make her run off.

Bandz stepped into Kalie's line of sight with a smile on his face. "How are you, Baby K?" he asked her as he squatted to try and meet her at eye-level. "Are you enjoying your surprise festivities?"

"Umm… yes, actually," she nervously spoke. "Bandz, right?"

"The one and only."

"Right. If you will excuse me, I have to speak to my sister, alone."

"No problem. But can you do me a really big favor?"

"That being?"

"Can you put my number in your phone? I'm going to need a session so that you can help me find out why it is that I have nothing but corny lines to give you."

Kalie caged her bottom lip between her teeth as she tried to conceal her smile. "Fine. But I have to have my payment up front. It's a hundred dollars per hour."

"I'm Bandz, baby," he chuckled, spreading his arms. "Of course I'm going to have your money up front."

"Okay," she giggled. "Put your number in and choose a date that hasn't already been chosen on the calendar."

Bandz was all smiles until he saw that she wasn't available until the week after next. "How about we do this over the phone?" he suggested.

"Cool."

He gave her a smirk, then left his number as promised. "Call me." With a wink, he handed her back her phone and left her there to speak alone with Sheena.

Kalie couldn't take her eyes off of him as he walked away with a limp. Sheena took her sister's chin within her hand and turned her face toward her. "Now, you listen to me, Baby K Devieux. You don't want to get that boy under your nose. You hear? Somethin' about him ain't right. He might be a little cutie. He might have money. You, however, are born from royalty. Nobody made you who you are. You did that. You don't ride coattails. He does. That boy only wishes that he could be Dolla. A man who can't be himself will only leave you confused and hurt, wondering who you are in the end." Sheena then released her chin and pointed at her. "You take my word. Mama ain't gonna like this either. You might as well do nothin' more than give him some sort of evaluation and keep it moving. Nothing more, nothing less."

"Sheena—"

"Nothing more… nothing less."

Kalie looked over her shoulder at Bandz and his crew, when she noticed someone other than him. She noticed Scrappy. His eyes were on the sun as it was falling behind the rolling waters, but there was something behind his orbs. She tilted her head in wonder at what could've been the matter. She was so focused on staring at Scrappy that she missed Bandz gloating to Legend about how he was going to get her.

CHAPTER FOUR

A Knight's Tale

On a Saturday morning, most people would be either sleeping late or trying to get their lineup ready for the week ahead. Edwin "Scrappy" Broadus knocked on the door of the shabby two-bedroom home where his daughter was being housed. When he didn't get an answer after fifteen minutes of knocking, he retrieved his cell phone from his back pocket.

Scrappy cautiously lifted his hand to the door and knocked again. When there was no answer then he decided to walk away. With his head hung, he marched over to his car sluggishly and looked down at his phone to see if he had any missed calls that he hadn't realized before. Maybe even to see if his ex had sent him any messages to let him know that she wasn't going to be home. Knowing her, that was far from what was actually happening.

"Where is she?" he asked aloud as Tamara could hear him loud and clear.

"She's gone!" a young girl shouted from the window of the house next to Tamara's.

Scrappy shook his head and slid off inside his car to drive away. He had no idea where he was going, but he had a bright idea of whose house he should visit next. On a whim, he went to Queenie's in hopes of finding Kalie. It was only on a hope and a prayer that she would be able to help him because she achieved her degree in psychology and would be able to help to piece him back together.

Scrappy didn't know what to expect. All he knew was that he was placing all his hopes in Kalie's hands. He knocked only twice to have a young woman open the door for him who assumed that he was there for Kalie. Without speaking to him, she immediately escorted him to the elevator and showed him to Kalie's room on the third floor.

The curvy, young woman left him there. He assumed that he was to knock. Sucking up his pride, Scrappy lifted his knuckles to the door and knocked. Nervous and all, he waited for Kalie to open. When she did, she looked up at him with shocked eyes.

"Scrappy, right?" she excitedly asked. "What are you doing here? How can I help you?"

"I... um... I know that you have your degree, so I was wondering if there was a chance that you could... *fix* me."

Kalie paused, trying to figure out what he meant. His handsome but saddened features told her that he was more than uncomfortable when confessing to needing help, but he was there and she had to do something. "Scrappy, I can't fix you, but I can help."

"What will that do?"

"It'll help you to help yourself. However, I don't have any openings—"

Flustered, Scrappy turned away.

Kalie grabbed the short sleeve of his shirt to pull him back. "Please. Stay. Consider this one on the house."

"I can't do that, Kay."

"Yes, you can. Come on."

Kalie's bright smile enticed him to accept her proposal of joining her in her bedroom for a quick therapeutic release. Contrary to what he wanted to happen, Scrappy put his walls up. She led him to her chair near the terrace, then took her own seat in front of her desk. Scrappy sank so far into the back of his mind that he couldn't hear any of the questions that she was asking. He couldn't hear her calling his name. The only thing that could be heard was the sound of his own heartbeat inside his ears as it escalated.

"Scrappy?" Kalie lowly called him. She gently touched his hand which sent an electrical jolt up his arm.

He flinched and took his covered eyes up to her. "Yea?"

Lightly she giggled. "How about I put the notebook away, and we do something else?"

"Like... like what?"

Kalie placed her composition notebook on her bed and sat on the floor with her back to it. "Tell me why you think that you need to be fixed."

"Umm... my daughter needs a father who isn't mental."

Kalie took a mental note of how he tapped his fingers on the wooden arm of the chair, and how his leg seemed to dance every time he spoke. This was hard for him. Extremely difficult from what she could see.

"Let's go over some small things, shall we?" she suggested. "What's your real name, where were you born, and what were parents like?"

Scrappy chewed on his bottom lip. He didn't want to have to do all of this or go through any of the painful memories, but for his baby girl, Phara, he was willing to. He cleared his throat. "My name is Edwin Broadus. The only reason they call me Scrappy is because I used to always end discussions with a fight. I was born here, in Little Haiti, just up from Wynwood. My parents? Umm… my mama ditched us when I was around four or five. I can't quite remember. My father… he's a different story in itself." He took a deep breath when debating on if he wanted to tell Kalie about how difficult it was growing up with his father. Like all things in his life, Scrappy swept it under the rug and surrendered. "Listen, I need to come back another time, alright? I can't do this."

"Don't give up on yourself—"

"I can't, okay?"

"Scrappy, you came here for a reason. You wanted help. It doesn't make you weak. It makes you stronger than any other person out there walking around with problems that aren't willing to so much as confess to needing guidance. Please? Will you stay?"

He stood and brushed his dreads to the back. "I really need to come back another time."

"Only to get yourself together, alright? I took you on, so now we have to finish together. I'm not a quitter, Scrappy, and honestly, I don't think you are either. The only way I'm letting you walk out of here is if you promise me that you're coming back." Kalie leaped up and rushed to her desk where she snatched up a business card that she had made before she left the north, then scribbled something on the back of it. Afterward, she handed it over to Scrappy with sincere eyes. "It's your appointment time. We won't be here though. Text me to give me your number, and I'll let you know what the location is."

Cautiously, he accepted the card, but he didn't look at the back just yet. He couldn't even find the words to thank her before he left. He sped off, taking the stairs to the bottom, and bypassed the girls who were coming into the house in their tennis wear. The senior of the girls eyed Scrappy as he whisked past and made a mental note to tell Queenie that he was there.

Finally in his car, and doing fifty-five miles per hour on Route-112, his phone finally screamed the lyrics to the song "I Hate You" by rapper Z-Ro. Angrily, he snatched it up and put it on speakerphone. "Oh, so now you know how to answer a goddamn phone, Tamara? Where the fuck is my daughter?"

"First of all, you won't be calling me with that kind of tone," she sassed.

"Bitch, I didn't call you! You called me! Where's my daughter?"

"If you get your shit straight, you would see that you blew my fucking phone up and that I'm trying to return said call. So chill the fuck out."

"Stop playin' with me and tell me where my kid is!"

"She's here at home, where she belongs. Where are you? Weren't you supposed to come and get her?"

"I was there almost an hour and a half ago! You didn't answer the door! Your neighbor said that you were gone!"

"No, I wasn't. I was asleep."

"Look, I'm on my way. Have her ready. Remember to put her inhaler in her bag because the last time you forgot it, we almost lost her."

"Yea, that's because you're irresponsible as fuck, Scrappy. You almost killed my daughter."

"Don't you fuckin' play with me like that, girl. Your forgetful ass didn't give her the fuckin' inhaler. Had it not been for me puttin' her in a full nelson, she would've suffocated. Have her together. I'm on my way."

Not long after he hung up, he was parking on the street in front of Tamara's small home. His nostrils flexed at the sight of his three-year-old sitting on the porch with her backpack on. Her white t-shirt was dingy, her navy-blue shorts were faded, and her sneakers were run over and muddy. Scrappy knew that he was handing Tamara a little over $2,000 in a month to make sure that she got what he thought she deserved, yet every time he picked his daughter up from her mother's, she looked as if she was a homeless and neglected child. What pissed him off the most was seeing her long and thick mane all matted in two ponytails.

Still, he got out and opened his arms for his daughter. He would always spend long minutes twirling with her on the small and unkempt lawn. Per usual, he took her to a small shop near Tamara's home to have her hair washed, pressed, and styled.

"Boy, one of these days, you're going to have to learn how to comb this baby's head," Ms. Jackson, the owner of the shop, joked as she took the hot-comb through Phara's dried and moisturized tresses. "But you know what? I ain't complainin'. That's money in my pot every weekend."

"Don't bust me up," Scrappy lowly said, while Stephanie, Ms. Jackson's daughter, twisted his dreads. She had already dyed his ends a light golden color, and now she was finishing him up.

"You need to take my advice, Scrappy. That girl comes in here three or four times a month to get her weave looked at, but the only time I see pretty Ms. Phara is when you bring her."

"She'll be back next week for braids," he returned, trying to let the subject go.

"That's fine and all, but you need to get yourself a lawyer before this baby goes bald because her hair is dying. It's so dry when you bring her to me, her ends are always split, and—"

"I'll ask for your written statement when I make my move."

Ms. Jackson placed the hot-comb on a heating station, pressed her balled fist into her pinched waist atop her rotund hips, and raised a drawn-on brow at him. "Pa pale ak chèf fanmi yo nan ki fason." With an attitude, she told him not to speak to his elders in that tone. "Jwenn sou travay ou tankou se te yon papa l 'ak pwoteje pitit fi ou yo." She reprimanded him by letting him know that he needed to do his duties as a father to protect Phara. "This girl is running around with your money and your daughter, and she doesn't do what needs to be done. I watched you grow up from a little boy in rags to a man with money at his fingertips. Ain't no reason that your child supposed to go around lookin' like this."

"Just say the word and that lil' bitch is gone," Stephanie said over his shoulder.

He dragged his hand down his face. "And this is exactly why you don't tell Haitians that you have an enemy."

"Of course not. Everybody knows that Haitians will get rid of somebody quicker than a Jamaican, without a plan, without gloating, and without mercy."

Ms. Jackson sucked her teeth. "Every woman in this shop knows that Tamara set you up to trap you and use you."

"That she did, Scrappy."

"Go and take your life back. You don't want to suffer for fifteen more years, do you?"

Obviously Scrappy had some thinking to do. Kalie helping was just step one.

———————

As soon as Scrappy pulled into the driveway of his small two-bedroom home, Bandz was calling. He huffed when hearing his homie's special ringtone. He looked into the rearview mirror to see that Phara was fast asleep with her long, black hair covering her cherubic face, and her pack of Starburst candy being held loosely in her chubby hand. He didn't want to answer, knowing that it was yet another party being held by Dolla, but he answered anyway.

"You know what today is," he grumbled.

"Yea, but it's important." Bandz sounded a little too excited. "Bring her with you. I'll call up a babysitting service to sit with her upstairs. Dolla's inviting that lil' muskrat from Cuba to talk business with him. Plus, he's tradin' off a few girls while we're there. Come on, Scrap. An hour max and you can go home with Phara. Besides, I want to see the little, pretty princess. You bein' real stingy right now, bruh."

Scrappy leaned his head against the headrest while weighing his options. He knew that Bandz was full of shit, but it was more money in his pockets so that he could take Phara as far away from her mother as possible.

"What time?" he asked under his breath.

"Ten is when we start letting people in. Be there around nine-thirty, so we can eat and jump fresh. Why're you acting like you're new to the shit?" Without another word, Bandz hung up, leaving Scrappy to look back up into the rearview mirror. Phara was his breath of fresh air. She was his sanity, and his reason for being.

He realized then that he would have to go ahead and open up as much as he could to Kalie. That way, he could get it on paper that he at least made an effort to receive an evaluation. When the shit hit the fan, he was already plotting on how to counter any and every possible strike that Tamara was going to throw at him.

––––––––––––

After kissing his daughter's cheek, he helped her into her pajamas and stuffed her hair inside her bonnet. "Behave," he told her.

"Oui, pére," she sweetly answered.

The young girl who was hired for only four hours popped her gum with a wide smile on her face. "That's so sweet," she commented. "You can speak French. Can you teach me?"

Phara animatedly nodded.

"You can go and get ready, Scrappy. She's in good hands. I'm just glad that she's not like the uppity, entitled kids that I look after the majority of the time."

"I want her in bed by ten," he informed her. "You can feed her, but nothing sweet. She already had a whole pack of Starburst. That's enough for her."

"I got you. Any allergies?"

"None. Just seasonal. But, oh!" Scrappy raced to the closet where he stored Phara's bag to retrieve her inhaler. "She's not to get worked up. She's a severe asthmatic. Any sound of wheezing coming from her, then you would only need two pumps."

The girl took the inhaler from his hand and rolled her eyes. "I have a little brother who has asthma. Trust me, I know how to use one of these. Go and try to enjoy yourself. She's okay."

Scrappy scooped Phara off her feet, smothering her fat cheeks in kisses. "You know that daddy loves you, right?" he whispered.

She nodded with her finger in her mouth.

"Good. I'll be back up here at ten o'clock sharp." With one last kiss, he placed her on her feet and headed out of the room. As always, he kept those large, sparkling light brownish-green eyes in his thoughts before working. She was always his push when he didn't want to work.

Scrappy went into the room he chose for the night and unzipped his duffle on the bed. With a deep sigh, he took his hung clothes to the bathroom in the hall to shower, shave, and throw on his attire for the night.

Dolla wasn't a man who believed that you could come to his meeting looking any kind of way. You had to dress the part. Scrappy buttoned his pressed, black slacks, then his white dress shirt, only leaving the top three buttons undone. Afterward, he slipped into a pair of black crushed velvet Italian driving loafers that had white embroidered crowns on the tops of them. His wrists were dressed in two sparkling bracelets and a watch that anyone would've killed to sell. Around his neck was a silver chain that had a diamond encrusted cross at the end of it. After three squirts of Perry Ellis 360, he was ready to try his best to enjoy himself while handling business.

Within thirty minutes, he was holding a flute on the concrete platform behind the house with each of his boys standing nearby. Clearly Dolla was in one hell of a good mood. He was wearing a smile that showcased the white diamonds in his bottom set of teeth.

"We don't have a meeting tonight," he announced. "Turns out that Pablo's grandson has two other nightclubs of his own, he has no problem in putting his wife over his grandfather's old spot, and he's eager to do business with us. He's expecting the first shipment tomorrow night. So, Flockas, let's make it happen."

Scrappy clinked glasses with the other happy men, but all he could think of was his percentage in all of it. The more money Dolla made, the more he received.

"Scrap, I need to talk to you right fast." Dolla flicked his thumb across his nose while waiting for him to come over so that they could take a walk around the Olympic sized pool. When he was close enough, Dolla threw his arm around Scrappy's shoulders. "You need to take care of old girl. She's doing some foul shit down there in Little Haiti. That's your territory, so you get that bitch axed, you hear me?"

"What you mean?" His face scrunched.

"I mean, she's out here hoein'. She got herself a pimp now. A nigga that I don't know. She wanted to come tonight to see if she could get a better one, but I told her that I had to talk to you first. I know you give this bitch money, but I'm guessin' that she's giving it to that no name ass dude she's fuckin' with. Set her ass straight, dawg. She got you out here lookin' real sloppy as fuck." Dolla gave him a pat on the back and left him there to think.

CHAPTER FIVE

Shit Happens

Kalie was uncomfortable in what Sheena chose for her to wear. She couldn't stop tugging at her skirt while going over her appearance in the tall body mirror inside her closet. Sheena had given her a white mini-skirt, a white halter top that exposed her tattooed back, and a pair of white and gold snakeskin heels that had a strap wrapped around the ankle. For her hair, Sheena flat-ironed it, gave it body, and combed it over onto one side. Her makeup was very light to give everyone the impression that she was not for sale but still had class. Kalie tugged at the opening where the neckline dangerously plunged down to her naval. The only thing holding the fabric together was a single gold chain at her bosom.

"Sheena, this is too much," she complained.

"Chill," she giggled from the bed. "They gon' try to buy you, but they know not to touch you. Mama don't play that shit."

Kalie whirled around to the bed with a confused face. "Mama?"

"Yea. She only goes so she can check out the competition. Oh, and she enjoys the cocktails while she's at it. Dolla hosts these parties quarterly. It's more income for him to seek out the best of the best and make trades there."

"Do you not understand anything you just heard?"

"Kay, calm down. If there's anything that I've learned from this lifestyle, it's the fact that medicine, drugs, and ass will always sell. Ain't no stock market crash from that shit. You can believe that."

"You bitches aren't ready yet?" Mocha complained from the door. She stuck her eyes on Kalie and gave her a once-over. With a smirk, she approached her little sister and folded her arms underneath her breasts. "Nice Louboutins, baby sister," she lowly commented. Then, she pulled open her long, white, sheer jacket that had black feathers on the lapels. Mocha stuck her oiled leg as her hands fit perfectly in the curve of her waist. "These are grown folks Red Bottoms." She nodded down at her pointy-toe black and white python skin, six-inch pumps. "Nice training wheels, by the way," she mentioned, making fun of the gold strap around Kalie's ankle. "See, you may try to look like me, little sister… but there can only be one Mocha Latte. And, oh yes… this is a body. You should try drinking more milk and eating more red beans and rice if you want to compete with this."

Sheena, with a brow raised, looked back and forth between her sisters, hoping like crazy that Kalie would stand up for herself.

"The funny thing about you, Michelle," Kalie spoke up, "is that you think that your own sister is competition. I'm not, darling. I'm just living. You should try doing that instead of creating an entire life wrapped around me. Red beans and rice? No thank you. Too much iron and starch. I don't need a body like yours. I spent too much time at the gym without a waist trainer and without having to ride a dick to firm up these thighs. You need to humble yourself, because right now, you look like high class trash to me."

"What'd you say to me?" Mocha took a step closer.

Kalie closed the space without any fear in her heart. "You heard me... Michelle."

"My name is—"

"Michelle. Mommy named you Michelle, so your name is Michelle. And the next time Michelle comes for Kalie, she had better get her motherfucking life. Find one if she has to. Little word of advice for Michelle... Don't. Come. For. Kalie." She blew a kiss at her sister, then sharply turned on the balls of her heels to get her white half-coat off the couch at the foot of her bed.

"Well, damn," Sheena commented. She got out of the bed and settled herself in her white, leather heels. "Bet that'll teach your ass that she's not a baby. Leave her alone, Mocha. Leave her alone." Sheena brushed off her white slacks and tugged at her clinging white jacket. For dramatic effect, she adjusted her bosom inside her fashionably visible white bra.

Mocha tightened her lips as Kalie and Sheena passed to leave the room. She didn't stop frowning until she had gotten inside her Mercedes jeep. She slammed the door and started it up with so much hate in her heart for Kalie that she was bound to do anything at her boyfriend's party.

Queenie got out of her Phantom with her long, black cane in her hand that had a silver lion's head on the top. She tilted her white Blixen then pulled her long, white jacket that squeezed her bosom and flared at the hips to let the wind catch it and blow it back. The animated lapels of her $1,500 jacket were made of black mountain bear fur. The dimple in her short, black necktie was a rhombus cut diamond that would make a baller want to slice her throat for it. Her silver heels were double platform peep-toes that she would only wear for this special occasion. They were handmade by one of her girls who had hopes of making her own mark in the fashion world. With the way she put together her madam's outfit of the night, when she graduated, her breakout success wouldn't be too far behind placing her tassel on the other side of her graduation cap. Any man in the room would take one look at Queenie and know that she wasn't a woman to be fucked with. She never needed a mister. She never had the need to depend on one either.

"Sheena," she lowly called her daughter over her shoulder. As soon as she smelled her daughter's sweet scent, she parted her ruby red lips and said, "Keep Baby K close. It's so many snakes in here tonight that I would hate to cut a few off."

"Yes, Mommy," Sheena agreed.

The man of the hour descended the stairs in his black, velvet sports coat, white slacks, and silver dress shirt. In one of his hands was a cigar, while a glass of brandy was in the other. Queenie cut her eyes at his black, crushed velvet loafers. Dolla was making more money than he was leading on.

"Welcome!" he said to the pimps and madam in his foyer. "I see that the selections are quite yummy tonight. Nobody spared anything, did they?" He chuckled.

Kalie, standing beside Sheena with her mother's two girls in front of her, leaned over to whisper, "How long is this going to take? I'm hungry."

"Oh, now you're hungry?" Sheena playfully nudged her sister. "He's just making an introduction. He'll be done in a minute, and then we can go off and eat some finger foods."

Even though Kalie nodded, she took in the fact that each crew was dressed in different colors to uniform themselves. Queenie and her family were dressed in mainly white, while Dolla and his folks were in black and white. There was an odd connection between the two high families.

When Dolla was done with his introductory speech, Mocha slithered from the crowd and hooked arms with her man. Dolla, on the other hand, had to step forward and kiss up to the rich woman who never spent money in his palace.

"Madam Queenie, it's always a pleasure," he said with a sly smile. "How much will you be putting out tonight? Zero? Or shall we try for at least ten grand?"

"Son." Queenie handed her cane to the girl at her left, then ran the stiletto nails on her index and thumb across the brim of her hat. "Two things in this world that I will never pay for. That's water and pussy. You should know that by now."

"Well, Mommy," Mocha spoke. "I'm sure that tonight you'll have a different opinion."

"And I'm more than sure you'll learn to speak when you're spoken to. Dolla, you should get you a lady who knows how to hold her tongue in the presence of real gangster. Daughter or not, you should really reinvest in someone who's not so fucking spoiled and only depends on her looks to get shit done."

"Madam," Dolla tried, but Queenie held up her hand.

"I wasn't done yet. And while we're on the topic of conversation that is the subject of looks. Your stable is lookin' kind of short. Are you having some issues, Dolla?"

"No, ma'am," he chuckled. "It appears that my greatest advisory has taken all the ripe selections." With the hand that was holding his cigar, he lifted Queenies hand and laid a gentle kiss on it. "I hope you enjoy the liquor this quarter. Last quarter was a bit of a dud, don't you think?"

"No, actually. The liquor was okay, but the bitches that were on the auction block could use some freshening up. My God, Dolla. Why do you entertain these weak ass men? It's almost like you're giving them false hope."

The rest of the conversation was drowned out when Kalie finally looked up from her shoes and laid eyes on Scrappy. He was more handsome than she thought he was. His dreads were freshly twisted, pulled away from his face, and they were braided into a ponytail behind his back. How could he hide such a chiseled, yet soft, face? His chocolate skin tone made her wonder if she licked his cheek would he actually taste like sweet coffee or hot chocolate. She was staring so long that she hadn't noticed Bandz approaching her or other people dispersing from the foyer and throughout the first floor of Dolla's grand home.

"Well, hello again, Baby K," Bandz politely greeted her. "Please, forgive me for coming on strongly when I say that you make me want to drop to one knee and propose to you in this outfit. It's either that, or strong-arm every nigga in this motherfucker for staring at you."

"What?" She shut her eyes tight and shook her head to try and understand what he had just said. She had completely missed it.

Bandz didn't pay attention to it. He took it as her nerves getting the better of her. It was her first time being inside his brother's home, so he based her zoning off as that. "You want something to eat?" he chuckled. "I'll take you to the good stuff."

"Yea, sure, I guess."

Sheena yanked his arm, pulling off her white framed shades to stare him down. "Behave yourself with my sister, or else I'll have your testicles for earrings; you got me, boy?"

"Sheena, relax," he told her with a smile. "Bandz is a good boy."

"Whatever. You heard what I said."

Bandz intertwined his fingers with Kalie's to lead her to the kitchen.

Scrappy's eyes temporarily raised from the phone he checked after receiving a hateful message from Tamara. When they had, he caught a glimpse of Bandz walking off with Kalie. She was completely different from how she looked earlier on in the day. She wasn't in her sweatpants and tank top like earlier. She wasn't in her colorful socks and had her curly locks flowing freely around her face. She was now in grown woman territory. She was a bad little motherfucker that made his jaws water. He swallowed his saliva and settled on the fact that grownup Kalie was cool, but he would rather her be the comfortable and down-to-earth girl who looked so innocent that she wouldn't utter a single harmful word.

Legend slapped his hand down on Scrappy's shoulder. "It's too many mommies in here for you to be over here worried about your baby's mama. Get you some ass, drink up, and live for a change, Scrap."

"What he said," Calmly agreed as he flicked his thumb across his nose. "Matter of fact, I plan on buying a few girls tonight, depending on how fresh they are. I ain't dependin' on this drug money and Dolla forever. Scrappy, let that bitch kill herself. Come on, homie."

"I'm with y'all, cuddy," Scrappy returned. "Too much ass out here."

Calmly and Legend walked off first, but Scrappy stayed behind to look over his shoulder at Kalie leaned against the island wearing a smile because of something that Bandz must've said to her. He shook his head, keeping in mind that a girl like her was way out of his league.

"So, you want to get out of here, right quick?" Bandz asked Kalie. "I just have the urge to kiss you so badly, man. Your lips are just so pretty, Kay. I can't help it."

"Does that work on all the girls?" she asked with a giggle.

"I never had to ask them because they weren't the asking type. Anything went with them. I just wanted to be a gentleman and ask you.

I didn't want to go for the kill and end up slapped across the face."

"You got that part right."

"I mean, we're both grown. I should be able to tell you how I feel with you."

"Let me take a guess." Kalie leaned off the island and strutted over to Bandz. Suddenly, she smashed her lips onto his with her hand slipping inside his slacks to grab his manhood. It was an okay size, but she had bigger. By the second, he was hardening in her hand. She pulled her hand out, locating the large kitchen pantry. "If you want it, I suggest you come and get it. You might not ever get this chance again."

Bandz's jaw slacked as he watched her sashay over to the closet. He didn't have a choice but to follow.

"By the way," she said as he closed the door behind him. "This is your evaluation. This is all you wanted from me anyway, wasn't it?"

"I mean, I wanted to get to know you—"

"Bandz… let's save all the dramatics and get right to the point." Roughly, Kalie unbuttoned his slacks, then pulled him by the shirt with a come-hither look in her eyes.

By the time Bandz dropped his slacks and briefs, he was so hard that if Kalie was as tight as a virgin, he was afraid that she would've snapped in half. Kalie lifted her skirt and turned away from him. She knew what he wanted. Since she hadn't had any in a while, she was willing, just to knock the kinks out.

Bandz placed kisses on her bare shoulder, sinking his teeth into her neck while he tore open a spare condom that he pulled from his pocket and fit it on. Forcefully, he moved her thong aside and pushed inside of her. Hearing Kalie's inward hiss almost drove him over the edge. Too bad that Kalie's wetness got the better of him after a few pumps. His knees buckled. Bandz was not only embarrassed but wondered what the hell had just happened. It was impossible for him to cum that quickly. No woman ever had the power to make him look a fool when he knew for sure that he was gifted.

"What's the matter?" Kalie asked him. She was ready for some kind of grand finale without knowing that it had already happened.

"Nothing," he lied. "Come here. I need to taste you."

She squinted in the dark. It hit her that he was a little too eager to taste her juices when usually men would ask to do that beforehand. Kalie whirled around and adjusted her thong. "Please. To be such a thug, you couldn't hang."

"Look, just stay for ten more minutes."

"Nope. Not interested. I told you that you might not ever get this chance again."

"Kay, I'm sorry. I swear that's never happened before."

"Yea, I'm sure it hasn't." She moved past him without caring if his trousers were up or not, and left after adjusting her skirt.

Bandz sucked his teeth with his eyes on his dick. He cursed it in his head. He truly didn't know what the hell had just happened. He more so couldn't believe that Kalie actually let him fuck. Maybe that's what got to him. He wasn't able to enjoy the thrill of chasing her. "Damn!" he cursed aloud, punching the wall at his right. Poor Bandz.

CHAPTER SIX

Merciless Prince

*A*t New Piman Bouk, off of 2nd Avenue, Kalie sat in her seat, stirring her sugar inside her glass of sweet tea while waiting for Scrappy to arrive. She had gone over the menu and figured that she had no idea what she was looking at, so she would rather let the native decide what they would eat for lunch on this day.

Scrappy shook his head at a Facebook post that was the subject of a screenshot that had been sent to his inbox. It was yet another post taking digs at his fatherhood. He would have to mash the gas on his plan to get Phara away from his conniving mistake that was his baby's mother. Tamara claimed in her post that he was trying to hold her back from making more income, yet he could walk around dripped in diamonds and designer clothes. It was quite clear that she wasn't the woman that he fell in love with four years prior. Had it not been for Phara, Scrappy wouldn't have been there during the nine months of pregnancy and the first year of her young life.

"Scrap!" Kalie happily called to him. "Over here!"

He looked up from his phone and bit his bottom lip to try and hide the scowl that he was doing his best to get rid of.

"Come on," she said with a giggle. "I'm hungry and I don't know what I want. Let's go!"

Scrappy licked his lips and pushed the thoughts of caressing her soft, glowing skin with his fingertips to the back of his mind. "What're you tryin' to eat?" he asked her as he approached the table.

Kalie immediately took her eyes back to the menu to keep them off of his solid chest through his white V-neck tee shirt. Her nostrils flexed at his scent. Goodness, he smelled like a manly man and it made her want to sink her teeth into his neck. "Umm... I don't really know what I want. I've never tried any of this before."

"You must be used to eating healthy food and going to the gym and shit, right?"

Kalie looked up while Scrappy was talking and caught a glimpse of his sparkling, gold teeth. He had a six piece set on the bottom, while his canine and first molar on each side was also covered in gold. "Umm... Uhh... yea," she muttered. "So, you choose. What would you recommend?"

"I don't even need to look at the menu to tell you that we're going to have plantains and beans, taso, and then Cassava for dessert."

"What's that? Like, I know what plantains are... but what is everything else?"

"Taso is Cajun barbequed meat. You can choose between beef, turkey, or goat."

Kalie's face scrunched. "Goat, Scrap? Really?"

"It's up to you. Cassava is actually a root. The dish is commonly called Cassava cake. It's made with cassava root, sugar and coconut milk."

"This is extremely unhealthy, but I'll take your word for it. Since I'm taking you out of your comfort zone, I can step outside of mine."

"Welcome," a young, chocolate woman greeted the two with her notepad and pen at attention. "What are we having?"

Kalie looked at her glowing phone on the tabletop while Scrappy told the woman their orders. She had a waiting message from Bandz. Just seeing his name on her screen made her want to laugh. It had been almost a week since the soirée at Dolla's, and it was the first time that Bandz had contacted her since.

"*Please answer my call,*" it read. "*We need to talk.*"

"*There's nothing to talk about, Bandz,*" she replied. "*Your evaluation was that you wanted to fuck. We did that, and now we're done.*"

"*Come on, Kay. Don't do me like this.*"

"*What's done is done. I'm blocking you now.*"

"So, my old man." Scrappy took the napkin off the table and laid it over his lap. "That's where we left off."

"Right." She nodded just after placing her phone on airplane mode.

"He was uhh… a hopeful man, you could say. After my mom left, he would drink, curse, beat the hell out of me… and repeat. This one time, I got so hungry that I was tempted to pop the top off of a barrel in the corner of our small kitchen. I waited until he left to do so.

When I popped the lid, I accidentally turned the barrel over. It took me forever to try and place all of that rice back inside it, but he came in and caught me. While he beat my skin to the white meat, he was yelling at me about how that barrel was given to him for good luck at his and my mother's wedding."

Kalie winced. "I'm so sorry, Scrappy."

"Nah, it's cool." He then cleared his throat. "After a while, I noticed how less abusive he was. He would sit on the couch like some sort of zombie. One day, I realized why that was. It was because he was using heroin." Scrappy flicked his thumb across his nose when trying to keep the painful memories coming. "At first, I was enjoying the fact that I had room to roam, but when he was sober, he couldn't remember a damn thing. After my first fight— I was about thirteen— he claimed that it was him that I wanted to duke it out with. I must've laid on the grass in our small backyard until the sunset that day. I just didn't have it in me to swing back at him. It wasn't right, you know?"

"Let me hit you with something hard. Why don't you talk a lot?"

He looked at her confusingly.

"I did my research on you." Kalie propped her fist underneath her chin with her smile intact. "Everybody that I've asked about you all said the same thing. They say that you don't speak, really. I appreciate you speaking to me, though. I especially love the fact that you're being so open with me. You're doing good."

"Well… at first it was because I used to speak really broken English," he honestly answered. "I used to mix Creole with French and English, and people could barely understand what I was saying."

"Really?" she squealed. "You're so country, though. That's hard to believe."

"Ou ta ka vle kwè mwen. Mwen ka fè prèske anyen son bon an kreyòl."

Kalie giggled. "What?"

"I said you might want to believe me. I can make almost anything sound good in Creole."

"Say something else."

"Ou gen yon booger yon ti kras pandye. Ou bezwen pran swen nan ke anvan manje a vini oswa lòt moun ou pral manje li."

With the baritone he used and the way he accented his words, he sent a chill up Kalie's spine. Her eyes rolled into the back of her skull as she squeezed her thighs together. "What did you say?"

"You have a booger slightly hanging. You need to take care of that before the food comes, or else you'll be eating it."

"Scrappy!" she gasped, turning away to grab her napkin to clean her nose.

"I'm just playin," he chuckled.

"Oh my God, that's cruel!"

The young woman returned with their dishes, sitting them onto the tabletop with ease. "Anything else?"

"Nah, we're good," Scrappy told her with a smile.

Even she had to lean back when she noticed that the corners of his lips had rose with his lips perched. She too knew that Scrappy smiling was not at all normal.

"I'm sorry, Kay. I had to prove a point."

"Oh yea? Well, next time, don't use my hygiene to do it." She was about to look up at Scrappy when her eyes stopped on the meaty dish in front of her. "Is that goat?"

"Sure is. You took me out of my comfort zone, so now I'm taking you out of yours. Eat up, yon ti kras mwen."

"What?"

"My little one."

Kalie rolled her eyes as she picked up her fork to sink her teeth inside of goat's meat for the very first time.

———————

Now, with her sandals in her hands, Kalie walked along the grass of the park near the shack where Scrappy grew up. She took in how fond the neighbors were of him, and how much respect he had. She couldn't wipe the smile off her face. A shopkeeper even stepped from behind his stand to hand Kalie a chopped mango. She accepted it and merely bowed at the elderly gentleman.

"Dous fwi pou yon ti fi dous." The shopkeeper returned her curtsy.

"What did he say?" she whispered to Scrappy.

"Sweet fruit for a sweet girl. You would say…" Scrappy leaned in closer to tell her what she needed to reply, just to hear her try his language.

Kalie cleared her throat. "Mèsi poutèt ou, marchands."

The elder grinned at her and sent them off with a wave.

"What did I say to him?" she giggled.

"That your mother looks like a goat."

"What?" she shrieked. Kalie whirled around, ready to take off down the street.

Scrappy pulled her along. "I'm just joking. You said, 'thank you, shopkeeper.'"

"That's not nice." Playfully, she socked him in the arm.

"Scrappy!" A young boy bolted across the street, dressed in what appeared to be a fishnet design of shirt that had the colors of the French flag on it. His long and untamed locks flew in front of his face while he went rambling on about something in Haitian Creole. He looked to be in a panic.

Scrappy stepped away from Kalie. Obviously, it wasn't meant for her to understand what they were saying because neither of them spoke the slightest hint of English. Curious, she pulled out her phone and hit the microphone icon on her Google widget to translate the language.

It caught on to Scrappy saying, "Pote yo ban mwen, epi pote yo ban mwen koulye a!" The words that came up on the screen frightened Kalie. *Bring them here, and bring them to me now!*

"Kay," he called her, almost out of breath. "I'm going to walk you to your car."

She was almost tripping over her bare feet with the way he was pulling her along. "What are you going to do?"

"It's just a part of my job, alright? You have to go."

"Scrap, I'm scared."

"Don't be. This doesn't concern you."

"No, I'm scared for *you*." Successfully, she yanked away from his grasp, running her fingers through her silky locks to brush them to the back. "Tell me what's going on."

"This isn't a part of the psych shit, okay? This is my job. I have to get you out of here, and I have to work."

"Tell me!"

"No! Now go!" With strength, he pointed toward the parking lot on the other side of the restaurant that they had enjoyed their meal not long ago.

Feeling small and shunned, Kalie folded her arms and stomped off to the BMW that she borrowed from Sheena. Once inside, she slammed the door, threw her shoes in the back, and checked her phone for messages since she had taken her phone off airplane mode and placed it on silent so that no one could disturb her conversation.

A call came through that made her nostrils flex. "What, Bandz?"

"Whoa," he chuckled. "Can you please bring all that beauty to the beach? South Beach, that is. It's a Saturday. I just want to get a chance to chill and relax before I have to go to work."

"Look—"

"Please don't say no. I promise that I will come and find you, and bring the fun to you."

"What is this about?"

"It's so that I can make up for how badly I embarrassed myself last weekend. I want to show you a better time. We have food, drinks, volleyball, and plenty of water to dip into."

"You get one hour, Bandz. Just one."

"You won't regret it."

Kalie had a feeling that she would regret meeting Bandz at the beach, but she went ahead anyway. It couldn't have been anymore worse than being yelled at and shown a monstrous side of someone that you could've sworn that you were interested in at first sight. She took off her white crop top before she had gotten out of the car, to expose her hot pink and silver polka-dot bikini top. She left her white denim shorts unbuttoned to tease onlookers with her matching pink and silver swim shorts underneath.

Bandz had just finished whispering into some girl's ear when he had gotten a message from Dolla. He warned him for the umpteenth time to stay away from Kalie. Like other times, Bandz marked the message as read, then sent a text to Kalie asking where she was. Lucky for him that she hadn't blocked him like she said she would.

"I'm behind you," she alerted him.

Bandz spun around on the sand with a crooked smile. Good Lord, that girl was perfectly toned. Her C-cup breasts sat alert in her bikini top. They made Bandz want to squeeze them.

"So, where's the fun?"

He ran his tongue across his lips while eyeing her perfect body. Just the thought of once being inside her almost made him bust all over again inside his swim trunks. "It's all here, baby."

For a while, Kalie actually enjoyed herself with two groupies who were trying to get close to Legend and Calmly. They played a nice game of beach volleyball with the girls versus the guys. After winning, and the guys cutting their losses, Kalie couldn't help but to laugh at Legend faking an injury in Spanish as his excuse for contributing to his and his boys' loss. Then, Kalie took a few shots off of Bandz's hardened abs. For only a split second, in the middle of going for her final shot, she saw the small tint in his swim trunks and smirked at it. He was like putty when being close to her.

"Kay, come with me," Bandz suggested.

She was now sitting on the sand near a pile of rocks, checking her phone for calls and messages from her family. "Give me a second, okay?"

"We're going to take the jet-ski. I've been having it for a while, but never used it."

Bandz headed off to his Yamaha WaveRunner with Kalie's eyes following. The first thing that came to mind was that it was dangerous. She had never been on a jet-ski before, but she was willing to trying anything once.

"*Where are you?*" Scrappy's message read.

"*At South Beach with your friends,*" she replied. "*Are you okay?*"

"*I'm on my way.*"

"Kay! Come on!" Bandz called to her.

She concealed her phone inside Legend's denim vest on the blanket where all of their belongings were, then skipped along to get on the jet-ski.

"I'll take it slow," Bandz joked.

"Shouldn't I have on a lifejacket or a seatbelt?" Kalie inquired.

"Just chill, baby. You're with me. Nothing will happen that's not supposed to happen. Hang on to me, and I'll ease you into it."

Calmly tapped Legend on the shoulder from the shore. He nodded in the direction of Bandz, who was going about getting out sea the wrong way. Calmly shook his head. "Queenie's about to skin his ass alive," he commented. "He's either about to kill that girl, or severely injure her."

Legend kept his eyes on the couple while he dried himself off. "This fool just doesn't know when the fuck to quit."

"On top of that, he knows that she doesn't want him. You can look at her and tell."

"You know that's not enough for this dumb ass. It's all in the thrill for him."

"Other than that, it's the money."

Legend looked back at him with thick pressing brows.

"Don't act like you don't know that he ain't gettin' no money from Dolla. If he gets Baby K, it's only because she's loaded. She's a goddamn princess. He can live off of her after he bags her."

"What's up, y'all?" Scrappy announced. He slapped hands with his buddies when he was close enough, then looked out over the waters to see Bandz and Kalie on the jet-ski. "What the fuck is he doin'?" he breathlessly asked.

"I can answer that!" Legend excitedly said. "He's getting ready to go into hiding after he snaps Queenie's daughter in half. Simple. She's about to kill his ass, and Dolla won't be able to sweet-talk his little brother out of that one."

All Scrappy could do was shake his head.

The trio watched as Bandz hit wave after wave. They could almost hear Kalie screaming from where they were standing. Scrappy stepped out of his shoes because of how rough Bandz was being with his vehicle. He could almost feel something bad about to happen.

Everybody saw the large tidal wave that was approaching, yet the show off that Bandz was, he didn't care to turn around or warn Kalie to hold on a little tighter. The three on the beach gasped when the jet flipped over and was swept underneath the surface. The only thing they could see within the blink of an eye was the bottom of the jet-ski aimlessly wobbling and floating away. First, Bandz broke the surface. The asshole didn't even look back to see where the hell Kalie could've been. He was much closer to the shore than his toy.

"Where the fuck is Kay?" Calmly shouted.

Bandz lost the feeling in his legs when he reached the shore. He couldn't answer because of water that built up in his lungs. He coughed, gagged, and spat out as much fluid as he could.

"Yo!" Calmly screamed as he beat Bandz's back in to help him get up the water. "Where the fuck is the girl? You're about to be one dead motherfucker!"

"Calm!" Legend yelled.

He looked up to see Scrappy pop up above water, almost thirty-feet away just to check his surroundings. When he dove back under,

Legend took off running to the nearest lifeguard's tower to get some help. No one was seated out, seeing as how there was another accident just yards away from where his group was stationed. He had no choice but to call 9-1-1 and pray that Scrappy could swim.

Bandz weakly stood to try and spot Kalie within the waves. His vision blurred when Calmly socked him in the jaw. He stumbled backward and held his jaw as if it was about to fall off. His fingertips were covered in crimson when he drew them away. "The fuck was that for?" he roared at Calmly.

"Because you're fuckin' stupid!" he returned, charging at Bandz.

Legend was able to step between the two in time so that neither of them would go to jail when the ambulance had arrived with the police.

"Did you even stop to ask the girl if she could swim, Bandz? Did you? What fuckin' idiot takes off on a jet ski without a life vest? Huh?"

"How was I supposed to know that it was a big ass wave comin'?"

"Dolla was right about you, fool," Legend told him. "Your ass don't think. Calmly... calm the fuck down. Scrappy went out there. Hopefully he'll bring her back."

"I'll go and get her myself."

Calmly pushed Legend out of the way. "Fuck that! You should've brought her back with you! What you gon' do when Queenie gets after your ass because you either killed, or almost killed, her daughter?"

"Ain't nothin' gonna happen!"

"Yo!" Legend had gotten both their attention and ran to the shore where waves were crashing against Scrappy's heels.

He was carrying Kalie over his shoulder before he gently laid her on the dry sand with Legend's help.

"Kay? Kay, can you hear me?" he asked her on his knees, patting her cheek.

Scrappy pulled off his shirt, then wadded it to place it beneath her neck so that her head would recline. He made Legend give Kalie chest compressions when he learned that she wasn't breathing.

For Calmly, it was the most agonizing minutes of his life to wonder where she was or if she was alive, then to stand by and watch as his friends tried to save her life. So badly he wanted to turn around and swing on Bandz again, but he chose to stand and watch in case they needed his help with anything.

"Goddammit, come on, Kalie," Scrappy mumbled while Legend pushed damn near all of his weight onto the girl's chest. One last time he pinched her nose, opened her jaws, and delivered air to her lungs.

She sprung up from the sand, puking dirty water in a daze.

"Thank fucking God!" Calmly managed to scream through clenched teeth.

Bandz ran over to her and slid on his knees to hug her. "Baby, I'm so sorry," he apologized. "I had no idea. Please, forgi—"

Kalie forcefully pushed him away and reached for Legend to help her up.

Scrappy quickly snatched up his wadded t-shirt, found his phone, and dipped. He didn't want to stay. He was too pissed off to try and hold a conversation of any kind. Kalie was too weak to try and call his name. She opted to throw her arms around Legend's neck.

"Walk me to my car," she hoarsely whispered. "My phone is in your vest. And can you please follow me home?"

"Sure, Kay," he answered. "I got you." He looked up and snarled at Bandz as he escorted the hurt and drenched young woman to retrieve her belongings.

"What's up with Scrap?" Calmly asked, following the two.

"The fuck if I know. Let's just be glad that he knew what he was doing. We all would be some dead motherfuckers."

CHAPTER SEVEN

A Knight With You

For the next few days, Kalie would have to make sure that her phone was on silent as to not disturb her, whether she had clients or not. Legend and Calmly had gotten her number from Bandz. They were relentless when making sure that she was going to be okay. She eventually blocked Bandz so that he couldn't get a call through. There was nothing that she wanted to say to him or hear from him. He acted very irresponsibly, even though she played her own part in it. However, Kalie argued with herself and told herself that she gave him a chance to see if he could be an adult for a change. Apparently, he couldn't be.

Today, since cancelling her only two appointments, she lounged next to the pool with Queenie at her side. The sun was very soothing. She needed to get a chance to relax for a while. Having back to back clients and looking at buildings to find her own office space wasn't very pleasing. It was exciting but tiring.

Queenie lifted her hat to look over at her daughter through the thick tint of her shades. Then, she adjusted the thick, white robe that she draped over luscious body, so that it would come all the way up to her neck. "Scrappy still on your mind?" she asked Kalie.

"Mommy, I swear I don't understand how he could save me and then just burn off," Kalie complained.

"I told you what it was, Baby K. It was Bandz being in the way."

"But I pushed him off!"

"He was already mad because you took your trusting ass out in that water with that ignorant, little boy."

Kalie bowed her head and slowly shook it.

"He still goin' through that bullshit with that girl from Little Haiti?"

She looked over at her mother in that moment with scrunched brows. "What girl?"

"His little girl's mother. The damn girl is out making him look bad every chance she gets. She ain't right. He needs better, Kay. He needs you."

"Mommy—"

"Ma!" Chocolate, the brunette who spoke to Kalie on a regular, called her. She was the senior of the house, and Queenie's temporary right hand. She was marching at a fast pace with a stack of papers in her tiny hand.

Queenie sat up, removing her shades from her face. "The hell wrong with you, girl? Don't you see that I'm relaxing?"

"Ma, it's an emergency," she informed her, handing her the pages. "I told you that girl, Blueberry wasn't going to last long here. She's making D's. On top of that, she's only bringing in $500 a night. The minimum is a grand. I have to pull rank. She needs to go."

Queenie flipped through the pages after removing the girl's report card from the top of the stack and skimmed through a paper the girl had due. "What the hell is this shit?"

"Exactly." Chocolate folded her arms under her breasts while adjusting her weight on the opposite leg. "She's not taking anything seriously. She's on the verge of losing her scholarships, and she's not even booking clients like she's supposed to."

"Give her a week of probation. Nobody told her to sign up for summer courses, so she's showing some kind of initiative. As I was saying." Queenie turned to Kalie as she slid her shades back on, not at all paying attention to Chocolate walking off. "This lil' girl is a thorn in everybody's sides. She makes him look like he doesn't do what he needs to do for his daughter. You can tell that he does though. His exterior might be hard, but you can tell that he's much more than what he appears to be. Poor Scrappy. He can do a lot better. Especially do better than he is with Dolla's sneaky ass. I think that it's great that you're speaking to Scrappy."

"Mommy, I saw another side to him. I almost have him figured out, though."

"Yeah?"

"He was so open last week. He was talkative, joking… He even smiled, Mommy. *Smiled.* You can look at him and tell that he doesn't smile."

"I told you that you were good for him."

"But, you meant it in a different way."

"Doesn't matter which way I say it or you take it. The point is that you're good for him. *Period.*"

Kalie leaned back on the lounge chair that she was very comfortable in. She took the moment to ask questions of her own. "What's the deal with Dolla?"

"What do you mean?"

"He seems…" Kalie shrugged. "Fake."

"This is how you know that you're my daughter. That nigga is as fake as a four-dollar bill. Mocha just looks at him like he's a damn god, with her stupid ass."

"Why does she hate me so much?"

"Because without effort you have done so much, but she has had to work hard and still ain't where she wants to be. Shit, you known how long she's been waiting for Dolla to marry her? Why marry a nigga when you're richer, smarter and better looking than he is? Now, if your sister put her mind to it, instead of hating you, then she could collapse his entire empire without batting a lash."

Kalie grabbed her phone and sent a text to Scrappy. She needed to see him soon. He never really gave her the opportunity to say thank you.

"You know," she said aloud as she typed, "the only reason that Scrap is seeing me is so that he can prove that he's sane? He says it's because he doesn't want his daughter to have a crazy father."

Queenie sucked her teeth. "Bullshit. That girl been sayin' for about two years now that Scrappy is crazy. He's probably just now believing her lying ass. She's doing everything she can to make that boy look bad."

"Why?"

"My sweet, sweet baby. Because that's what crazy, scorned ass bitches do, honey. They try to use their kids as leverage."

"That's stupid."

"It is, but it's smart on their part because they break the men in that way. That girl keep fuckin' around, though, and Scrappy is gonna end up chokin' the shit out of her."

Kalie chewed on her bottom lip while thinking of how to get Scrappy to open up about it.

Almost as if she could hear her daughter's thoughts, Queenie said, "I'm gonna have to take a trip downtown and pull a couple of strings to help this man get his child away from that crazy bitch. He doesn't deserve any of this."

A lightbulb went off over Kalie's head. She would have to ease him into the conversation and talk about his issues with his kid's mom.

———

Kalie sat Indian style on the sand with her hands tucked between her bare thighs. Being in front of the ocean was the only time that she could be the most comfortable. Today, she dressed in a pair of short swim shorts and a bikini top. Her hair was crinkled, laying over one shoulder. Though it had plenty of volume, her holding spray was able to prevent her strands from falling in her face.

"What're we doing here?" Scrappy asked as he sat on the earth next to her. He hugged his knees, staring out over the water that rushed in mere feet away from them.

"What do you see when you look out there?" she replied. "When you look at the earth around you and the water?"

He lightly shrugged. "I see crystals," he lowly answered. "How the sun dances off the water. It looks like little diamonds." Scrappy took a deep breath and removed his hood to make Kalie a little more comfortable. "What'd you see?"

"Life. It humbles me."

"It's... calming," he hesitantly revealed.

"How so?" Finally, Kalie looked over at him to notice, for the first time, the square-shaped diamonds in his ear. There was one on top of the other. Scrappy even had a nose piercing. A small, diamond stud that was hardly noticeable.

"If you just listen to the waves... follow them with your eyes. It has a way of vexing you but creates something so calm within you."

"Why vex, Scrappy?"

"Because when the sun sets just right... it's so beautiful. So many elements and so many vibrant colors create something so beautiful. You want to be a part of it, but you can't. It's too much for one person to handle."

"How?"

"You would drown, Kalie. Everybody knows that."

"Is that why you don't indulge in conversation? Because of the many elements and so much coming together that you think it'll be too much for you to handle? You don't want to drown within it."

"What's this really about?" he asked, becoming flustered with the many questions. "It's not a secret that I saved your life here. Is this why you brought me back? So that I could relive the only time I've stepped outside of my shell? And for you?"

"I actually wasn't thinking about that part, but look who just made a connection of their own."

"Look, Kalie… I don't think you can help me, alright?"

"We've come this far. What makes you want to give up?"

"What makes you want to keep trying with me?"

"Because you are a challenge, my good sir," she announced with a grin. "I'm learning more about you than I have from any other person on this planet. When you let me into your mind, Scrappy, I can see so much that everybody else is forbidden to see. Honestly…" Kalie shrugged as she leaned forward to grab her ankles. "I feel kind of special," she said lowly with her eyes on the rolling tides.

"I gotta go."

"Scrappy, my mama knows about your daughter's situation," she suddenly blurted.

He looked over at her through lowered lids.

"Oh, come on. All of Little Haiti knows about that girl and how she's keeping your daughter away from you. I should let you know right now that my mama always gets what she wants, and she's going to get your daughter for you."

"I don't need your help," he said through caged teeth.

"Well, you really don't have a choice in the matter, now do you? My mama sees the good in you. She knows that you're being done wrong, and she's pulling every string possible to bring your daughter home."

"Then tell her to ease up!" Scrappy leaped off the sand with a hardened face behind his curtain of locks.

"I can't," Kalie said matter-of-factly as she looked up at him. "I don't know what you want from me. You asked me to try and help to fix you, and that's exactly what I'm doing. That little girl brings a twinkle to your eye, as does any daughter to their father. So, yes. I'm standing behind my mother on this, just so that I can try to help to get you where you need to be."

"Fuck this," he said beneath a breath. Angrily, Scrappy stormed away from their spot to head to his car in the lot.

"Sometimes we can't do everything on our own!" Kalie bellowed. "Sometimes it's good to get help!"

To him, the Devieuxs were sticking their noses in business that didn't concern them. He thought better of Kalie, but if she weren't careful, she was going to end up just like her family— thinking that they knew and owned everything.

CHAPTER EIGHT

Not In The King's House

"Lady, you're not hearing me!" Bandz yelled while pacing the floor of his bedroom. With his cellphone up to his ear, he was more than livid after checking the process for his package. "It was supposed to be there three fucking days ago. Today is Friday! Do you know what that means? Well, obviously, you don't. You're fucking incompetent. What's the point in paying for express delivery, if... What? Woman, I can't understand shit you're saying to me! Is there anybody there that can speak fuckin' English?"

"Pitiful," Dolla mumbled from the bedroom doorway. "Can't even get a package delivered."

Flustered, Bandz hung up and tossed his cellphone onto his platform bed. "Then *you* get it delivered! Why do you ride my fuckin' back so hard, man?"

"Because I need you to do better. In doing that, I need you to stay away from Baby K."

"Why?" He pulled up the legs to his heavily starched jeans and sat on the foot of his bed.

"Because you fuck up everything you touch. I have a plan for her." Dolla lit a cigar and patiently waited for a decent blaze. Then, he puffed his tobacco, releasing thick clouds of smoke. "I'm going to launch Kalie into being one of the best damn psychiatrists in Florida. With her comes medical distribution. You know how much money motherfuckers make in legit pharmaceuticals? And if I can get my hands on it, I'll be one made motherfucker. What do you think I've been doing with these pills at these nightclubs? I have niggas waiting and watching to see what they do to people. How do you think we'll get into the FDA? Money, Bandz. All it takes is money. They don't give a fuck how badly these medications fuck people up, they just want the money. So do I." A wicked laugh erupted from Dolla's pit. "It's all going to go through the champion Baby K. She'll be prescribing them my miracle drugs. Of course they're going to come back to her for more."

Bandz didn't find anything funny. For the first time in his life, he felt bad for what was happening around him. "You're using Kay? *My girl?*"

Dolla waited until he had cleared all the smoke from his lungs before he spoke nonchalantly. "What good is she to anybody? She's good to you for a fuck. She's good to her mama because of her golden pussy. She's good to me because of what she can do for me."

"Why don't you just use Mocha? You been porkin' her for the last seven years."

"And what good has that done for me? Hmm? Besides track her mama's every fuckin' move and to calculate what Queenie's going to do next? She's a complacent bitch, just like her daughters. But Kalie? Kalie wants better. She's hungry for more. She has a fire for her need to help others. Well, she can help me."

"That's fucked up," Bandz mumbled.

"What's fucked up is the fact that you still don't see the bigger picture. That bitch, Queenie, still makes at least seven million more than me without even taking her morning piss. This is a win-win for me, simply because I get two of her daughters under my belt, and I earn more than she ever will. I'll be untouchable, Bandz. Un-fucking-touchable."

Bandz bowed his head. He wanted to throw up the fact that his brother wasn't the only one to get two Devieuxs at his fingertips. Bandz just so happened to have fucked them both. Maybe it didn't come with money and lifelong luxury, but it was something that Dolla couldn't accomplish.

Later that night, Bandz could hear how roughly his brother fucked Mocha. It didn't drive him crazy, yet it made him reach out to Kalie from a different number. He poured out what little of his heart that he had to her, and expressed how he felt for her. He made sure to mention what a great couple they could be together. He even went as far as humbling himself just to try and win her over again. He only hoped that it would work.

Surprisingly, he received a message from her. *"I don't know anyone that would try this hard, but I will give you one chance and one chance only to meet with me face to face. This is your last opportunity to wow me."*

He slid his phone underneath his pillow with a small smile on his face because he was getting a chance that he wasn't sure that he deserved. Yet, Kalie would complete him in a way—whether financially, socially, or emotionally. A tender knock came at his door that he wasn't expecting. He hadn't had the chance to tell his late-night caller to enter before Mocha stepped through in her black, laced bra and panties.

"Fuck you doin' in here?" he asked her. "Take your ass back to Dolla."

"Come on, Bandz," Mocha told him in a sultry voice as she closed the door behind her. "Finish me off. You know I can't leave until you work me off."

"Mocha, get the fuck out." He tucked his arms behind his head and stared up at the ceiling from his bed.

"Got my little sister under your nose, huh? You know she ain't a grown woman."

"Get the fuck out, or else I'll call for my brother."

"What is he going to say? That you fucked his girl, and then kill you?" She sashayed over to the bed, climbed upon it, and straddled him. "You know you want me, Bandz. You can stop faking it for a change."

"The only reason you want me is because your sister has me. Get real."

"She can't have you." Mocha placed soft kisses onto his bare chest, which hardened his nipples. In her mind, her sister was no competition. Especially when pleasing Bandz. "You're mine," she said to him in airy words between kisses. "I want you so badly." Mocha began to grind against his silk pajama bottoms, knowing that Bandz could feel her warmth.

"Mocha," he moaned. "Get the fuck off me."

"I need you, Bandz. You know that." Slowly, she descended to his knees, so that she could fish his manhood out of his briefs and bottoms.

———

Kalie couldn't sleep with the vibrating of her phone beside her pillow. It was the number that Bandz had texted her from. She squinted at it, wondering why he would be calling so late. She cleared her throat and answered, but all she heard was rustling. That was before she heard the smack of skin, moaning, and someone who sounded very familiar cry out, "Bandz! Fuck me!"

Quickly, Kalie hung up and tossed her phone over onto her nightstand. "Disgusting fuck," she grumbled. How could he call her and have the audacity to lay up with someone else? "Weak ass."

Her phone went sliding across her nightstand. This time she was equipped to answer and record what she was hearing so that she could throw it up in his face when need be. However, it wasn't his number. It was another. Her heart sank. Maybe one of her clients had an emergency. "Kalie Devieux?" she answered.

"You have a collect call from… *Scrap*," the automated system told her. "Will you accept the charges?"

"Yes!" Kalie whipped the covers off of her and stood out of the bed. While being patched through, she waddled to her closet in case she needed to throw something on. "Scrappy! What happened?"

Two hours prior...

Scrappy was livid. Tamara had been ignoring his calls all day. He was tired of the games she played when it was time for him to get Phara. Angrily, he hopped out of his car, leaving the top down, and banged on her front door. He didn't give a damn if he ended up breaking the door down. He was going to get in and get his daughter, by any means.

Furiously, Tamara swung the door open with her hand on her hip. Her hair was wrapped up in a leopard skin printed rag, her makeup was meekly done, and her nightgown was one out of a catalogue. "Why the fuck are you beating down my goddamn door like the police?"

He didn't answer her. He moved her aside and stepped into the messy place. Shaking his head at the strewn food wrappers, clothes, and plastic food containers on the floor, he ventured inside Phara's room, where she was laying on her stomach on her bare mattress. The only thing she was dressed in was her panties. Scrappy took his phone out and took a few photos of his daughter's room, which also smelled like urine.

"What the fuck are you doing?" Tamara yelled from the door. "You ain't gon' come in here and take pictures of shit for your new bitch! Nigga, you don't do shit for her, but you think you got a right to judge me or my house? I got to go to work, take care of her—"

"You ain't got no fuckin' job, hoe!" he roared.

Phara flinched, covering her ears.

"Fifi, go to your closet," Scrappy told his daughter. "Go now."

Obediently, Phara hopped off her bed and briskly traveled inside the closet, where she closed the door.

Scrappy pushed Tamara out of the room, slamming Phara's bedroom door behind him.

"Don't put your hands on me!" she complained.

"Bitch, I ought to knock your ass out! How the fuck you got my daughter lookin' like this, but you all over Facebook, tellin' motherfuckers that I don't do what I need to?"

"Because you don't! What I put on my page is what the fuck I put on it! Who gon' stop me?"

"Why do I always have to play these games with your stupid ass just to get my kid, man? When the fuck are you goin' to grow the fuck up and act like an adult about shit, Tamara? I get her hair done every time I come and get her. It looks like shit within a seven-day period, because your dog ass doesn't pick up a comb to at least attempt to do something to our daughter's head. On top of that, I keep her laced, but your stupid ass send her to me in rags. What the fuck are you doing with her stuff?"

"You don't do a bitch ass thing for Phara! Don't come around here, actin' like you give a fuck!"

"Are you stupid and retarded at the same damn time?" Scrappy grabbed at his dreads to keep himself from putting his hands on Tamara. "How the fuck do I not do for Phara?"

"Scrappy, fuck you. You know you don't do shit for her. Why you're running around here pretending that you do? You're trying to tell everybody that I'm crazy and shit. I'm on to you, nigga. That's why you wouldn't let me go to Dolla's party. You want me to be beneath you—"

"Do you know that bitches would kill to see two stacks a month in child support, Tamara? I still send my daughter home with money, just to make sure that she has what she needs. You still got to run out here and act stupid. Look, we ain't together and we never will be."

"Because of the new little prissy bitch that was with you at the spot?" Tamara closed the space between them as she worked her neck at him. "Yeah, you were all comfy cozy with the proper light skinned hoe; laughin' and talkin' and shit. You better not ever let me catch another hoe around my daughter, or else you won't ever see her again, nigga. You're lucky that my nigga let you take her now."

"What?"

"You heard what the fuck I said."

"You got another nigga that I don't know, around my daughter?"

"He ain't none of your business with your broke ass. And you want to know how else I know that you don't do what the fuck you're supposed to be doing? Because Phara calls him daddy."

Scrappy couldn't contain himself. Before he could think of his daughter, he pushed his phone inside his back pocket and wrapped his fingers around Tamara's throat. He shoved her back against the wall in the hall, lifting her above the height of his shoulders. At that point, he didn't care if he snapped her neck. She would be one less worry in his life, and a major weight would be lifted off his shoulders.

Instead of suffocating her, he tossed her into the living room as if she wasn't a whole one hundred and eighty pounds. Tamara crashed into the side table near the couch, rolling over a lamp that had fallen over with her.

"You still want to play with me?" Scrappy shouted. He almost stalked her every roll as he slowly strolled down the hallway. "Get your bitch ass up and face me, Tamara! You want me to be a nothin' ass nigga to you? You want me to look bad? Bitch, I'll help you make me look like a fuckin' monster."

"No, Scrap!" she cried.

He grabbed the back of her neck to lift her from the floor, then threw her over onto her love seat. "You got my daughter callin' another nigga her daddy? Huh?"

"Scrappy, please!" Tamara put her hands up to block him if he decided to hit her.

"Père! Père!" Phara called him. "Père! Venez me chercher, s'il vous plaît!"

He slowly backed away from Tamara, even though he wanted to do more damage, because his daughter screamed for him to come and get her.

Scrappy pointed at Tamara with a clenching jaw and flaring nostrils. "You fuck with me some more, and I promise that I'm going to finish your ass off, girl."

Then, he went to the closet to retrieve his little one. She had shimmied into a pair of dirty shorts and a t-shirt. Scrappy picked her up and left the house with her. Not long after he parked inside his own driveway, two cop cars pulled up on the street. One blocked his car with the other behind that. The cops got out and drew their pieces on him.

"Let me see your hands!" one cop yelled at him. "Make it nice and slow! Where's the girl?"

"My *daughter* is in her car seat," he returned with disgust.

The cop nodded at the other to head over to the car to make sure that he could see the little girl in mention who was supposedly kidnapped.

"It's clear!" the second cop informed him.

Scrappy sucked his teeth. "My top is down, man. It wasn't hard to see her."

"You Edwin Broadus?"

"I am."

"Place your hands behind your back."

"For fuckin' what? Bringing my daughter home?"

"You are under arrest for the assault of Tamara Dade, and the attempted kidnap of a minor."

"That's bullshit!" Scrappy spat while the officer wrangled his wrists in cuffs. "How the fuck can I kidnap my own kid, man?"

"You have the right to remain silent. Anything you say, can and will be held against you in the court of law."

"Well, use this: I didn't kidnap my own fuckin' daughter. I have her on the weekends. Even her mama can tell you that. This is all bullshit! Fuck y'all!"

CHAPTER NINE

Unveiling Deceit

With Sheena on her heels, Kalie went up to the central desk inside the police station just so she could get some answers. Dressed in a grey sweatshirt that was cut off at her bosom, a black cami underneath, and a pair of fitting black shorts, Kalie wasn't so sure how she would've been taken by her appearance alone, but she was on a mission.

"Kay."

She turned, with Sheena, to see Legend there with his hair in two ponytails, hanging over the shoulders of his black t-shirt. In his hands was a cup holder with four cups of coffee in it.

"Legend, what's going on?" Kalie almost panicked. "All he told me was to get out here as his psychiatrist. He said for me to keep calm and wait for the sheriff."

"He'll be a while. They did a shift change about an hour ago. Take some coffee and have a seat. He'll be out shortly."

"But, Legend—"

"Kay, trust me. It ain't Scrap's first run in with the law. Just try to have a little patience." He reached the holder out to her for her to finally accept a cup from it. "It's all black. How I like it." Legend then threw a wink at Sheena.

"Kalie Div... Div-ox? Div—"

She rolled her eyes at the young Hispanic woman behind the desk. "It's pronounced Divi-O."

"Whatever. Down the hall and to the right. The sheriff will see you now."

After following the instructions, Kalie came face to face with a pot-bellied man who was busy laughing it up with a few police officers to notice her standing there. She cleared her throat. "Excuse me? Sheriff?"

"Sheriff Jackson," he chuckled. "You must be Devaux."

"*Devieux,*" she corrected him.

"Yeah. Your client is in there." He pointed with his fat, pink thumb over his shoulder to the door at the side of him.

Kalie had just about enough of the lack of respect from the people of the law. She had to remember that she was in the corrupt land of the sound. Still, she pushed on to get to her client.

Scrappy was pacing inside the twelve-foot by twelve-foot room in only his white muscle shirt and jeans. He had long surrendered his shoes, jewelry, wallet, and cellphone. When he heard the door open, he slightly turned his head with his face scrunched. He looked like he was about to rip somebody's face off until he recognized Kalie.

Her eyes welled after seeing him pacing and prowling like some wild, caged animal. She knew that he had to be at the end of his ropes. Because of the mirror behind him, she refrained from wanting to grab his face and lay a kiss on it that she had been plotting to do for quite some time. Instead, she pulled out a chair and sat at the steel table, hoping that he would follow her lead.

He did. Scrappy, out of all the time he was in holding, finally started to feel bad. Kalie's aura wrapped around him and made him feel some sort of human again. With one hand balled inside the other, he rested the back of his fists against his lips with his eyes on Kalie's cut off hoodie.

"Scrappy, I want you to be honest and open with me," she lowly said to him. "How are you feeling?"

"Like shit," he hurriedly returned. "I just wanted my daughter, Kay. That's it. She had to play games and talk to me like I wasn't shit, when all I wanted to do was get my daughter for the weekend that I was promised."

"Did you hurt her, Scrappy?"

The door to the room swung open. A young, white male stepped through with greased auburn hair, a pressed suit, and a Hermes briefcase in his hand. "That'll be enough, Edwin," he announced. "Kalie, your mother wants you to get home, immediately. I advise you to give her a call. Edwin, we're leaving. Now."

"Who the fuck are you?" Scrappy asked with a scowl.

"I'm Charles Cohen. I'm your new lawyer."

"You mean you're my mother's shark," Kalie commented. "Well, you're right on time, I can tell you that."

He tossed Kalie a smirk, then handed Scrappy his card. "Prepare to go to court, Edwin. Just one hearing and your daughter is yours. I've already filed a restraining order against this Tamara Dade on your behalf. You'll get to see your daughter in the morning."

"Damn," Scrappy breathlessly said. "Queenie doesn't fuck around, does she?"

"Not at all, son. You're taken care of."

Kalie stood and so did Scrappy. They both exchanged handshakes with Charles before taking their leave.

"Umm, won't you need my notes, if you're going to court with him?" Kalie asked.

"Not at all, sweetheart," he chuckled. "I've already started on making him look like a saint. Oh, and here are your belongings, Edwin." Charles sat his expensive briefcase down on the table, bringing out Scrappy's jewelry, wallet, and phone.

"The fuck are my sneakers?" Scrappy complained.

While the others spoke amongst themselves, Sheena sat with her legs crossed, almost losing her patience. Legend was seated four chairs away until he decided to swallow his pride and move over to sit right next to the Amazon herself.

"Excuse you," she scoffed.

"Sheena, how long are we gonna play this game, huh?"

"I'm not playing games. Move."

"I got somethin' for you."

She eyed him with a raised brow. "Is it somethin' my mama can use? If not, it ain't valuable."

"You know I'm crazy about you, right?" Legend licked his lips with his eyes on Sheena's gorgeous face. Even when she was scowling, she was beautiful to him.

"Boy, you're just crazy in general."

"Sheena... I ain't a snitch or nothin', but you should know that Bandz is into some foul shit."

"That ain't got nothin' to do with my mama or the family business."

"But, baby, it's more valuable than you could ever know."

"First off, don't call me your baby. Secondly, spit it out or get your ass back in your seat."

"Fine." Legend got down on one knee in front of Sheena, grabbed her hand off her thigh, and kissed it. "Bandz been stealin' money from Dolla. I think the only reason he's after Kay so bad is because he wants to get away from Dolla so tough. You should hear how Dolla talks to him. He thinks that we don't hear him, but we do, babe. Bandz doesn't think. If we're not careful, he's going to do something that not only he's going to regret, but we will too because we didn't see it coming."

"Still—"

"Kalie got to stay away from him. You know like I know that when Kay got home and Dolla was all over her with that Welcome Home bullshit, he wanted something. People don't accept his kindness without something big in return."

Sheena's eyes were hooded behind her lids. "What do you mean?"

"I mean, because he was so called nice to Kay, then expect her to be hooked on some kind of contract soon. We done already got rid of Juan Pablo."

She snatched her hand away as she uncrossed her legs from shock. "Greasy motherfucker downtown with the pink and purple ass club?" She couldn't believe what she was hearing.

Legend nodded. "I went in all big and bad ass shit, Calmly followed suit… but it was our usual routine to get Dolla's money out of motherfuckers. Bandz was the one to pull the trigger."

"What?" she asked breathlessly.

"He didn't shoot Pablo until he started talkin' about Bandz pinchin' off Dolla's money by an extra ten percent."

"Legend, why are you just now telling me this?"

"I couldn't piece it together until me and Calmly started talkin' about this fool, Bandz, the day Kay almost drowned."

"Do you have any idea who Pablo is connected to?"

"Baby—"

"He was hella fuckin' important to my mama's trade." Sheena was damn near hissing in order to keep her voice down.

"He was?" Legend's neck bucked back.

"His bullshit ass grandson told us that it was a robbery."

"His grandson has gone into business with Dolla."

"Sneaky, sneaky, sneaky sonofabitch." Sheena leaned back in her seat as she tapped the tip of her pointer finger at the base of her chin.

"What is it, baby?"

"Boy, I am about to knock your ass out if you don't stop calling me that."

"You might as well get used to it because I'm not going to stop. Plant those pretty hands on my face and I will lovingly accept the painful bruises and scars afterward. All for you, my Amazonian goddess."

"Legend—"

"Why the fuck are you on your knee?" Scrappy asked.

Legend hopped up and kissed Sheena's hand. "Haría cualquier cosa por ti, mi amor."

"¿Qué quieres decir?" Kalie asked.

He had told Sheena that he would do anything for her, in which Kalie responded by asking what he meant.

Legend's head whirled around to her. "You speak Spanish, mujercita?"

"I do," she replied with a giggle. "What's going on?"

"What's up, Scrap?"

Scrappy slapped hands with him, pulling him into a manly hug. "Queenie pulled a bad ass white boy out of her vault for the kid. Looks like I'm doing well."

"Speaking of which, we need to talk. Me, you, and Calmly."

"About what?"

"About Dolla."

"What about him?"

"Do we want to fuck around and get caught off in the Queen's wrath when she finds out what's going on...? Or do we want to keep working for a man who would rather throw us under the bus once he gets a new business venture?"

"I'm lost, like for real."

Sheena cleared her throat as she stood. "Baby K, it's time for us to go."

"No," she politely opposed. "If it's okay with Scrappy, I just want to make sure that my client gets home safely."

Scrappy took a step back to look at how innocent Kalie appeared to be. He knew that she was lying. Her entire demeanor was a little too sweet.

"I just want to make sure that you're okay mentally. That's all."

"Yea, okay." He flicked his thumb across his nose, then took off for the front doors.

"Well," Sheena sighed. "I guess you'll be coming home with me, Legend. Besides, you have some explaining to do with my mama."

Carelessly, Kalie followed Scrappy out to Legend's car, where Legend tossed him the keys.

"I'll be back in the morning for my shit," Legend told him. "Wish me luck. I might become a daddy tonight."

"In your goddamn dreams!" Sheena shouted.

"And good God, aren't they so vivid and nasty?"

"Come the hell on with your nasty ass!"

Kalie covered her mouth to keep from laughing.

As a gentleman, Scrappy opened the passenger side of the money green Lexus LS460, VIP style. Kalie slid in onto the gold-colored leather seats and hugged herself while she waited for a barefooted Scrappy to get in and head to his home. She wasn't nervous as of yet, more like she thought that she was slick. Scrappy crank up the car and immediately shut off Legend's sound system. His boy always listened to his music louder than anyone else he knew.

"You good?" he asked her.

She threw a smile on and happily nodded, though she wasn't happy at all. She was more worried than anything. Her phone buzzed in her back pocket. She didn't care to answer as of yet. It would have to wait until dawn.

It only took Scrappy a little over twenty-minutes to arrive at his home. After shutting off the engine, he opened Kalie's door for her, then helped her out. With haste, he unlocked the gate that covered his front door, then shoved his key inside the two locks that he had installed on the front door for safety purposes. Kalie didn't have time to get a good look at the place once Scrappy flicked on the light to illuminate the living room. He had turned around to softly grab her jaws, forcefully lying his lips on top of hers.

CHAPTER TEN

Unfit For The Heir

*D*olla stirred on top of his gold silk sheets. The air was thick and something was ringing in his ear. It took him a while to gather that it was his phone. He ignored it. Dolla rolled over in bed to find that Mocha hadn't stayed the night. Because of the vacant space next to him, he opened his eyes and sat up with a grimace. She knew damn well that he hated it when she didn't care to stick around for the next morning's activities before he would send her on her way.

Angry, Dolla snatched his phone off his black marble nightstand and leapt out of bed to head to the master's bathroom. He noticed his missed call from Calmly, so he returned it while draining his pipe.

"What's up?" he asked Calmly.

"Did you know that Scrappy was knocked yesterday by that bitch, Tamara?"

"What? What the fuck for? What did she do now?" If Dolla couldn't be more angry after waking up, he was certainly there now. Nobody was to fuck with the Flockas. They were too valuable to him. Especially Scrappy. He could easily mentally maneuver through anything while the other two did the footwork. He couldn't count on his little brother to get the job done, but the other three were his prize. To have them on his team made Dolla comfortable with sitting still for a little while. They were more than competent. They were his knights in a foolish game for the kingdom of Miami.

"She claimed that he beat her up," Calmly explained. "She even pressed a kidnapping charge on him."

"What the fuck?" he roared.

"Yea."

"If you hear from him, tell him don't worry about shit. I'm gonna send my lawyer down there. That bitch got to go."

"Oh, don't worry about that part. Queenie already fixed the situation. She took him a lawyer and posted his bail."

"She what!"

"Yep. He should be home by now. I just thought that I should let you know. If he doesn't work for a hot lil' minute, then that's why. He's getting his head together. Oh, and you don't have to worry about his head. Baby K went home with him, so he should be straight."

"Good… Good girl. That one there is valuable."

"Who? Kay?"

"Hell yea." Dolla shook his dick, then flushed his golden toilet. He only hoped that the running water from his swan-neck faucet wouldn't distort his call while washing his hands. "Keep her safe, Calmly. We need her."

"You would think that Bandz knew that shit when he tried to kill her ass last week."

Dolla's phone fell to the floor from between his head and shoulder. Quickly, he shut off the water and fetched a thick, black and gold towel to dry his hands so that he could pick up his phone without a possibility of it malfunctioning. "What the fuck did you just say to me?"

"I *said...*" Calmly animatedly cleared his throat on purpose. "Your reckless ass brother almost killed her."

"How?" Dolla's face contorted so badly that if his face was made of stone, it would've cracked.

"That jet-ski you bought him last year for his birthday? He put her on it without a damn life jacket. This fool chased a wave, and it flipped over. Thank God that Scrappy knew CPR or else she would've—"

Dolla hung up and slammed his phone against the lavatory. He was steamed. Dolla couldn't compose himself in the right amount of time that it would take any normal man to just take a breather and regroup. He found himself bursting into his brother's room.

Bandz shot up with wide eyes to see what the matter could've been.

"I stood here and told you how fuckin' valuable Kalie Devieux was to me and you almost killed her?" Dolla shouted.

Bandz tilted his head from confusion.

Dolla stomped over to him and grabbed him, dragging him out of the bed. Lucky for Bandz that he landed on his feet. As if he was a woman, Dolla took a strong backhand across his brother's face. When

Bandz leaned over, he must've broken inside. He grabbed a lamp that he didn't even remember buying. With the neck held strongly in his hand, it only took one mighty swing of it, for the base of the lamp to connect with the side of Dolla's head. He hit the floor with a loud thud, but Bandz wasn't done.

"I'm not your goddamn boy!" he shouted, swinging the lamp at his brother's neck, shoulders and the back of his head. "You don't fucking own me!"

Dolla flopped on the floor, trying his best to crawl away from the assault.

Bandz circled his brother until he was at Dolla's head. With his bare foot, he kicked his brother's shoulder to make him roll over onto his back. Then, with the neck of the lamp resting against his neck and shoulders, he squatted to meet Dolla at eye-level. Nonchalantly, he swiped his finger over a gash at the side of Dolla's forehead, and inspected the crimson on his fingertip. "Damn. It's funny how I ain't lookin' at my own blood on my fingers for a change. Now what you're going to do is leave me and my business the fuck alone."

Dolla spat in Bandz's face.

With the back of his hand, Bandz wiped the gloss away from his chin. "That's the wrong fuckin' answer, big brother." He then tossed the lamp and stood tall to walk into his closet. "For a man who always complains about thinking, you fail to remember that I know everything about you and your dirty little operations. If you try to come after me, or try to kill me, I'll revert to being meek and weak baby brother, go to the police with everything I know, and then accept the consequences of your mighty hand. But by then, you'll already be in cuffs. Stupid motherfucker." Bandz ripped an outfit down off a hanger, then took it to the bathroom in the hall.

Dolla lazily picked himself up off the floor. His brother needed to be taken down a peg or two. How dare he threaten his kingdom when he was the one who was playing foul with Dolla's future investments?

———————

Legend adjusted his specs on his face after Calmly pulled his cell phone away from his ear. "What he say?"

"That nigga's pissed," Calmly chuckled.

"He should be."

"I'm not gettin' caught up in his bullshit."

"That's why we're here, isn't it?" Legend turned away from Calmly's round body Mercury, leading the way to Queenie's tall double doors.

Sheena opened them with a scowl on her face. She had plenty of time to get herself together in her mother's home. It could've been the fact that Legend was spitting straight facts hours prior about him chasing her, that she already knew of, or it could've been how her mother hated to see a woman who didn't care to put herself together before the day began. Her face was beat for the gods, and her attire for the day was only a pair of skin-tight jeans, along with a designer baggy tank top made of silk. At the age of twenty-seven, she had no kids. Her only job was keeping the books for her mother and scouting new business ventures. Sheena was the protector of Queenie's enterprises, and she took her job very seriously.

Legend looked down at her perfectly manicured toes in her sandals and smirked. "Damn, you got some pretty feet."

"Shut up." She rolled her eyes. Sheena personally escorted the two young men to the gazebo beyond the pool so that they could have an early breakfast with Queenie to discuss everything that Legend had told Sheena hours prior.

Once they were seated and plates had been made, Queenie sucked the juices from her peaches off her fork, with her eyes slicing through Legend's. "What the fuck makes you believe that I would trust you?" she asked seriously.

"Queenie, everybody knows who you are," he explained. "Me compared to you would be like comparing a host of a restaurant while I'm just a busboy. I have to do what I have to do to protect Little Havana. Those are my people. They'll get caught in the cross-fires of all this bullshit. And for what? For one man who's greedy enough to snatch up what he can and not give a fuck about the people who got him what he has in the first place? No. My loyalty is to the people. Dolla may pay alright, but my money came from Little Havana before he picked me up to squeeze money out of others. I won't have my home destroyed by a woman who's also protecting herself and her family. Make no mistake, I'm more than prepared to protect myself and my people in the event of that happening, but it's not fair to anybody at this table that we're all being used as pawns."

Sheena couldn't take her eyes off of Legend. The way he spoke was so different from how he usually was. She was used to him bouncing off the walls and being such an asshole that she wouldn't dare touch him or try to get to know him. Now, he was a grown ass man, speaking so passionately for his home and his people that it turned her on.

"So… let me get this straight." Queenie dabbed the corners of her mouth with her napkin, then placed it back at her lap. "Bandz steals money from Dolla, Dolla wants to use my baby as income, and Bandz pulled the trigger on my Juan Pablo?"

"That's exactly what it is."

"Consider you and Little Havana safe from harm. You're free to go. That is, unless Calmly has something that he wants to contribute."

Calmly removed his shades to sit them on the table. What Queenie admired about both twenty-two-year-olds was the fact that they needn't look at one another for reassurance.

"His empire is already crumbling," he said. "I refuse to be a pawn in his game when trying to rebuild it. For years, I was side by side with my boys, trying to make sure that his shit was straight and his hands were clean, but I ain't gonna get rolled over by no bus when he's caught assed out. There was no reason for Pablo to take a bullet, but his blood ain't on my hands. Lastly, you shouldn't treat the people who keep you up like they're beneath you. Whatever happens just happens." That said, Calmly grabbed his shades off the table, and stood to leave the grounds.

Legend grabbed Sheena's hand to kiss it before taking his leave with his old friend.

"That boy got it bad for you," Queenie commented while watching Legend walk away.

Sheena couldn't even return a statement. She, instead, propped her elbow onto the table and rested her cheek against her palm. A small smile slowly crawled across her face.

Sheena was so far inside her thoughts that her facial expression couldn't change when her older sister came marching out of the house with her mug on mean. In a pair of slides, Mocha was stomping wildly with her cheeks puffed.

"And here comes the Wicked Witch of Dade County," Queenie complained with her forkful of egg whites at her lips.

"Don't start with me," Mocha angrily spat. "What the fuck were the stooges doing here, Mommy? Why were they in this house?"

"Shit, with the way you talk, you could've sworn that you paid a goddamn bill around here."

"You shouldn't trust them." Mocha plopped down in a seat across from Sheena, folding her arms over her fitting muscle shirt.

"Is that what your man told you?" Queenie laughed, just before shoving her eggs into her mouth. "No, you shouldn't trust a man who plays in your pussy for seven fucking years and won't put a ring on your finger."

"Mommy, what were they doing here?"

"That's none of your business. Why haven't you put yourself together, Michelle?"

"Mocha," she corrected Queenie.

Queenie picked up her bread knife and pointed it at her oldest daughter. "You ever correct me again, and I'll cut you from cheek to cheek." She then directed the edge of her blade at Mocha's backside.

"Now, you speak to your mother like you have some respect, or else I'll redecorate your whole build. You got that, *Michelle?*"

"*Mommy*... Legend and Calmly don't belong in this house. I'm just looking out for you."

Sheena's eyes finally rolled to the front after she took them off the doors. She had been staring at them as if Legend was going to come back to make her laugh or say that he loved her. Now, Mocha made her want to choke her.

"Tell me something," Sheena perked. "How many times have you sucked Dolla's dick with no information to bring back to our mama?"

"What?" Mocha sneered. "Why are you worried about my man's dick?"

"Because you had a fuckin' job to do, Mocha. You were supposed to get under his nose, infiltrate to check out the competition, but then you up and fell in love with the nigga."

"Why is that your business?"

"Because Mommy's business is my business. You were supposed to do a job, and you failed. You failed so hard that I bet you didn't even know that Bandz damn near killed Kalie. Not only that, but he fucked around and shot Pablo because he's stealing from your man. On top of all that... your man is trying to use our little sister for his own benefits."

Mocha's face was riddled with red. She knew about everything else except for Bandz stealing money. *The spiteful little brat,* she thought.

"Or... is it that you knew and just didn't have the gall to speak up about it because you let dick come between you and family?"

"She came in here dressed in sweatpants, still reeking of cheap cologne," Queenie laughed. "You know damn well that she doesn't know anything. By the smell of her, she wasn't with Dolla. He has too much class beyond everything to smell like that."

"What's your problem with me?" Mocha snapped, slamming her hand down on the table. "You act like nothing I do is ever good enough for you!"

"Because it's not," Queenie said matter-of-factly. "I didn't raise you to be so whiney, forgetful, hateful, and spiteful. Hell, look at Sheena. She does what needs to be done for the family, and she's just fine."

"Single as fuck with no kids." She rolled her eyes and sat back in her seat.

"Then there's Kalie. You know, the one you hate so fucking much."

"Yea, well, had I been born just thirteen years later, I'm sure that you would've spoiled me too."

"That's your fuckin' problem, right there. You don't deserve to be spoiled. Yeah, you made your own money, but it was off of what I taught you that helped you to get that. Everything else I taught you just flew out of the window."

"Well, what did you teach Miss Perfect?"

"That she shouldn't be a fucking cry baby. Instead, go for what she wants, slay the fuck out of it, and claim what's hers. The same damn things that I taught you and Sheena. And for the record, I love how you're gettin' off the subject. Did you or did you not know about the shit that was happenin' with Dolla? You damn sure ain't reported shit to me. Like the fact that my right hand in this fuckin' trade was gunned down by your stool's boy."

"How was I supposed to know that, Mama?"

"It's Mommy, and you should know because you're fucking him, Michelle!"

"Oh, so now you're hurt because you can't put anymore hookers on the street who aren't fit enough to go inside your luxurious house?"

"You know goddamn well that that's part of the reason that I'm furious!"

"And the other part is because you loved Juan."

"You had better take it real easy with the road you're trying to walk on, little girl. I do what I have to do in order to keep this family fed. What I do doesn't need to be looked down on by anybody. One more foul word out of you and I'm gonna start redecorating your ass."

"Well…" Mocha stood and tugged at the ends of her t-shirt. "It's nice to see that you loved her and her daddy more than you loved me and mine."

Queenie's nostrils flared as Mocha strutted across the yard and around the pool. She wanted so badly to chuck her knife at her own daughter, but she expected for Mocha not to understand.

"You think she'll tell Kalie about Pablo?" Sheena asked lowly.

"Knowing her hateful ass, she just might, so she can try and break her."

"What do you want me to do, Mommy?"

"Take a break, Sheena. Let Mommy clean her own ass for a moment. Go and do something with your life, like linking up with

Legend. You don't want a good one to get away, do you?"

Sheena looked at her mother with sorrow in her eyes. Her mother and Pablo's love story was one for the books. Two completely different people from two seriously different worlds. Had terms been different, Sheena had no doubt in her mind that her mother would've been married with a stable full of ungrateful and hateful stepchildren, but she would've had real love. It was the only reason that Sheena was afraid to fall for anyone. Legend wasn't like Pablo, however. He had his shit together, he knew what he wanted, and he was going after it. But Sheena felt the need to always protect her mother after Queenie seemingly had gotten rid of a piece of her heart just to set Pablo free so that he could work without the possibility of a threat coming his way. Why Pablo was working with Dolla was a mystery. One thing was for certain. Queenie was stronger than Pablo on any given day, and she always taught her girls that your man had to have equal strength or stronger. Anything less was a dead deal. Because of this, she saw it in her best interest to seek out Legend just to see what he was about.

CHAPTER ELEVEN

Breaking The Shackles & Chains

Scrappy could barely sleep. After kissing Kalie, he backed away from her and went to his hall closet where he pulled down an extra blanket and pillows. He showed her to his room, where he would allow her to sleep for the night, then made up his couch so that he could sleep on it. Neither of them were paying attention to the knocking Sandman. After a while, Kalie left the room and sat on the floor with her back against the couch, where he lay with his ankles crossed and one hand behind his head. To get him to open up once more, she opted to tell him about herself.

"Growing up with my mama wasn't easy," she confessed, hugging her knees at her chest. "It was trivial, but it had its advantages. Like, being the baby of the family, you have a lot that you have to live up to. Mommy didn't expect you to cry. She didn't expect you to step outside of your bounds unless it was necessary. She damn sure didn't expect idiots for girls."

"Then, one day, she sent me away. I was ten. I wound up in Philadelphia in an all-girls Catholic school for those who were more superior in intelligence. I hated Mommy for that. For some reason, I wanted to know why, and in knowing her, I knew that I couldn't just come out and ask. So, I did some digging of my family history over several phone calls. It turned out that my grandmother was a wife to a pimp. Can you believe that?" she giggled. With a brush of her loose strands that came out of her tight, balled up ponytail, she pushed through her back story.

"Grandmother thought that it was fair to introduce my mama to the game when she was just thirteen. Selling her virginity would've put a lot of money into the house since my grandfather's girls were all drugged out and only making a minimum of fifty dollars a night. Along the lines, Mommy didn't think that it was fair for her to pull in so much money but never see it, so she ran away at age sixteen to start her own hustle. Uneducated and all, Mommy was making some serious loot. I'm not too sure about what else she had her hands in, but I knew that introducing her own two daughters to it was something that she didn't really want to do, so then it came down to me. Mommy had to break that chain of family sex slavery, which is why she sent me away. And you know what? I understood the method to her madness. I was highly fortunate not to have to endure what Mocha and Sheena went through before she was able to get enough riches to pull her daughters off the selling block."

"Why are you telling me this, Kay?" Scrappy grumbled.

"Because I know that as a parent, you have to do things that you know you're going to regret, but it's for the better. My mama opted to only see me over the holidays for twelve long years, just so that I could have better. She kept her dirty deeds away from me so that I wouldn't have to see them. She kept them away so that I would understand them when I was old enough to. That's exactly what you're doing with your little one. Also, you're not crazy Scrappy. It's just that unconditional love will make you do some crazy things."

"My old man," he said, chewing on his bottom lip. "He, uhh… he hasn't seen me in years."

"Is it because you hate him, or is it because you're not ready to face the past?"

"Kay, you don't have to do this anymore. Your mama's lawyer has me straight."

"I don't have to do a lot of things." She stood and turned to Scrappy with an unreadable expression on her face. Suddenly, she straddled him on the couch, with her arms loosely hanging around his neck. "Tell me, Scrap. Which is it?"

"I'm not ready," he answered honestly.

"Because of what you went through, you don't want your daughter to go through it. Life gives you two options when dealing with the past. It can either make it stronger, or either you can continue the sins of the past. You're in the same boat with my mama. I think that's why she likes you so much. She can see it in you. She believes that you're meant for much more."

"Kay—"

"You don't want the help because you feel like you've made it this far on your own. Scrappy, you're a good man."

"No, I'm not."

"You are. No matter how much you or society may see you as different, it's true. Just look at how far you're willing to go to keep the balance in Little Haiti. You sent me away so that you can handle business. You're willing to go to prison for your daughter, because that's exactly where you were going to be headed had my mama's shark not come in time."

"Kay—"

"I see it, too." Without waiting any longer, Kalie decided that it was best to finish what they started.

Lovingly, she gently brushed Scrappy's dreads away from his face to see his unique, blue eyes. Then, she hungrily kissed his lips to let him know where his place was with her. Scrappy accepted her kiss and gave in to temptation. He didn't give a fuck how badly Bandz would've been pissed off when he found out about he and Kalie. He was more than prepared to deal with the temper tantrum-throwing man.

Scrappy's large, strong hands moved up her bare thighs, squeezing her luscious backside with wanting. Kalie's tongue brushed across his own. It made him hard underneath her. The only issue they had were that their clothes were in the way. Scrappy leaned up only for a moment to help Kalie remove her shorts and thong. Not long after, their lips were sealed again. Kalie's small hands assisted in helping Scrappy to undo his belt buckle and button. Once it was finished, Scrappy hurriedly freed his dick and introduced it to Kalie's center.

Her inward hiss was worth it. He wanted to apologize for being so rough, but he couldn't. He placed kisses along her neck that made her shudder. Her legs quivered with every stroke until her walls had adjusted to his size. It had gotten to be so intense, that Scrappy had to take off his muscle shirt, tossing it elsewhere for the time being. He loved the fact that Kalie was so toned and fit because she was a light-weight. He could pick her up or move her how he pleased. For now, he grabbed her waist, leaving her bottom half hanging over the edge of the couch. Then, he helped her to take off her cami and sweatshirt, finding that she wasn't wearing a bra. Her breasts were perfect enough to sit in such thin fabric without a bra to shape them.

Eagerly he grabbed one, guiding the other into his mouth without using his free hand. He wrapped his tongue around her waiting nipple, then nibbled it just a tad. Hearing Kalie's moans and screams made him want more of her body. Her fingers were getting tangled within his locs, yet he didn't mind at all. He thrusted deeper inside of her, feeling her wetness soak his pole.

"Scrappy!" she called him with a quaking voice. She was close to cumming for him.

He sat back on his knees, running his free hand along her washboard stomach to flatten it so that she would feel him more.

The only thing to ruin the moment was his cellphone singing Legend's ringtone. That didn't stop him. He dug deeper into Kalie with a twirl of his hips. When she put her hand up on his abs, Scrappy took it down and shoved it up to the side of her head with their fingers interlocking. Over Kalie's pleas and cries because she had already unfolded, was the sound of Scrappy's home phone ringing. Still, he hadn't answered. He continued to drive Kalie crazy with slow, deep and meaningful strokes, along with his soft kisses to her collarbone.

The answering machine to his cordless phone near the plasma over the fireplace sounded. "*Your call cannot be answered at this time. Please leave a message after the tone.*"

BEEP!

"Scrap!" Legend screamed through the speaker. "Nigga! Guess where me and Calm at!"

"We're at 120 Northeast 150th Street!" Calmly said, all too excitedly. "We know you can hear us, man! Pick up!"

"Pick up the phooone!" Legend sang. "We're about to be knocking on the doooor!"

"You goosin'? Huh? Is ya'? Pull out, nigga! We're on the way with some heavy shit."

"Booyah!"

BEEP!

As if his friends weren't clowning around on his answering machine, he sacrificed his orgasm by slowing his strokes to a regrettable stop. With his nose, he turned Kalie's face by her chin so that she could look at him. For a few seconds, his face only hovered above hers so that he could stare into her angelic face for a moment. Kalie was biting her lip so hard that she was damn near about to bite it off.

"It's not hard to find the shower," he grumbled. "Handle your business and then go to my room. I'll take you home after they leave."

Even though she looked as though she was about to cry, she nodded to comply.

Slowly, Scrappy pulled out of her, then helped her up by her hand. Instead of just sending her on her way, he held her in his arms for a moment. He couldn't help but to slightly bend down and kiss her lips, with her standing on the tips of her toes to receive it. She fit perfectly in his arms. Everything about her made him feel so human and so alive again. He didn't get that with Tamara. He thought that he would have. He thought that she would understand him, but all she understood was his money.

"I won't take long, I promise," he whispered against her lips.

Kalie pecked his lips once more, then set out to find her clothes.

At the first bang of the gate, Scrappy scurried into the kitchen to rip a piece of paper towel off the roll, wet it, and took it over his rod to get rid of Kalie's residue.

"Open it up!" He heard Calmly bellow as he banged on the gate.

"Oooh, Scrappy, right there!" Legend playfully swooned, imitating what Kalie would've sounded like. "Yes, big boy! Hit that spot!"

The Spanish duo busted out laughing at themselves.

Scrappy pulled the front door open and leaned against the pane of it with his head tilted. "You do know that y'all are childish as fuck, right?"

"Man, we just fuckin' with you," Legend laughed. "For real, open the door."

"What's the password?"

"Open the fuckin' door?"

"Good enough." Scrappy unlocked the gate from the inside to let them in, exchanging their signature handshakes as they entered.

"Oooh, you were goosin'!" Legend said, pointing at the messy sheets on the couch.

"Man, this nigga was obviously goosin' his-damn-self." Calmly waved him off as he ripped the sheets off the couch. "It don't even smell like a woman's been in here."

"Shows how much you know. He could've sprayed some of that air neutralizer shit before he opened the door."

"You're puttin' too much thought into my sexcapades," Scrappy chuckled. He plopped down on his love seat and hiked his feet up on his coffee table. "Why are y'all here? It's like nine in the morning."

"*Wrong!* It's damn near ten-thirty. And we're here because we just left Queenie's. Tell him, Calm."

Calmly flicked his thumb across his nose to run down everything that was spoken of and to give Scrappy his own interpretation of how things were going to go down.

Kalie had just stepped out of the shower and wrapped a towel around her body when she saw her cellphone glowing near the sink of Scrappy's properly decorated bathroom. It was Sheena's number on her screen. She hurriedly dried her hands to answer before she would have to hear her yelling.

"Hey, sissy," she greeted her.

"This isn't your sister, my little beauty," Queenie said.

"Oh, hey, Mommy. Is everything okay? I meant to return your

call—"

"It's fine. I'm sitting here with Sheena, and I decided to give your line a ring. Listen, I'm giving Sheena some time off, so things are about to get a little hectic. I need you to come home as soon as you can. Where are you, my love?"

"I'm, umm… at Scrappy's."

"Good girl. I'm sending a car to you. You will be able to come home now?"

"Umm… yes, Mommy. Are you sure that everything is okay?"

"I'm sure. We need to have a little grown up talk. Just me and you. Be ready in about fifteen minutes. If the address that the lawyer has is correct, the driver should be to you very soon."

"Okay," she nervously responded. "I'll see you soon."

Queenie hung up, leaving Kalie to look at her folded clothes on the toilet. She could only wonder what was happening. She hadn't done anything out of the ordinary besides stay the night somewhere else.

Kalie took her time to comb out her tresses and left them in the curls that the steam from the hot water caused. Then, she located the extra toothbrushes Scrappy stored underneath his sink. She brushed her teeth, going through every possible scenario of what she and Queenie could've had to talk about. Finally, she dressed and left the bathroom.

She could hear the guys from the living room throwing jokes back and forth at one another, but ignored them to fetch her sandals from Scrappy's bedroom. After putting them on, she looked at the clock on his Cherrywood dresser and saw that her driver was supposed to be outside already. She grabbed her phone and made her way down the hall to get to the front door.

"Kay!" Legend loudly called her.

She stopped in her tracks, looking as if she had been busted.

"Nah… you don't look pregnant yet."

Calmly busted out laughing, slapping five with Legend.

Scrappy threw a pillow across the room at him. "Chill, man. Kay, don't mind them. They always get like this when we're alone."

"She gon' have to get used it," Legend said. "My boy got his fangs into you, so… you family now. Well, you were already my family, 'cause your sister been my wife for five years. She just didn't know it."

"Ooh… kaaay," she awkwardly sang as she approached the back of the love seat. With a soft hand, she ran it down Scrappy's chest and rested it there, placing a gentle kiss on his cheek.

"Where are you goin'?" he asked. "I thought I asked you to stay in my room."

"I know," she sighed. "My mommy needs me. She sent a driver for me. Whatever it is, it must be important."

The sound of a car horn honking verified what she thought; that the driver was there and was ready to take her home.

"I'll call you, okay?"

He lightly nodded.

What she noticed was that his dreads weren't hanging as such a veil would over his face. His features were exposed. She liked him like that. Again, she kissed his cheek, not caring that the other two in the room were well aware that Bandz wanted her. He could kiss her ass for all she cared.

Scrappy had gotten up and escorted her to the door. He tugged at the belt loop of her shorts for her to turn around one more time. When she had, he had to steal yet another kiss from her lips. It made Kalie blush once she pulled away.

"Is this nigga in love?" Calmly commented.

Scrappy waited for Kalie to get into the SUV and pulled off before he closed the door. "Fuck you, Calm," he said with a smirk. "I might be. Who got somethin' to say about it?"

Legend threw his hands up and crossed his legs as such a woman would. "No one. No, sir. Not me. Not saying a damn thing."

A bang came at his gate.

Scrappy rubbed his chest with his bottom lip caged between his teeth, thinking that Kalie couldn't resist and made the driver turn around. Happily, he pulled open the door to see the last person that he expected.

"Let me in," Bandz said anxiously.

CHAPTER TWELVE

Fuck You, You And You

Scrappy's brows squeezed together. "Fuck you doin' here, Bandz?"

"A nigga can't come and check on his homie?"

"Check on me, for what? What reason could you possibly have—"

"I ain't ever got the chance to thank you for saving my girl's life, plus—"

"Your girl? The one who pushed you away when you almost drowned her?"

"Look, that was an accident."

"Yea, well, what's not an accident is me closing the fuckin' door in your face, you greedy motherfucker."

"Greedy?"

"Yeah, nigga. You thievin' ass nigga. You killed an innocent man who was gonna cough up the dough. In turn, you got me and the others in the middle of some shit that we have to get ourselves out of. But don't you worry your selfish ass head about us. We were good before you, and we're gonna be good after you. Oh, and Kalie? You damn sure ain't got to worry about her. She's in good hands. Now step before you catch somethin' hot in the chest."

"You're threatenin' me?"

"Nah, nigga. I'm promisin' you." With that, Scrappy slammed the front door in his face.

Bandz stepped off the porch without a single thought as to where he would go. It appeared that his boys were on to him and the walls were closing in. But what the fuck did Scrappy mean by telling him that Kalie was in good hands? Was he fucking his girl?

"You gon' get yours!" he shouted. "All of you niggas!"

———————

Kalie walked into the house with her sweatshirt tied around her waist. Chocolate was coming down the hall near the stairs when she stopped her. "Your mom's in her office," she said out of breath.

For the first time, Kalie stared at her curves in her workout attire and admired her figure. Kalie gathered that an extra meal or two wouldn't hurt anything. Maybe a southern guy like Scrappy wouldn't mind a little extra meat on her bones. For now, she had to push it to the back of her mind to see what her mother wanted at a time like this.

Into the lavish office, she had gone to get whatever this was over with. Queenie sat behind her white, Victorian-styled desk with her legs crossed. Kalie shyly entered where she knew that her mother would be barbaric with whatever she was about to say.

In her hands, Queenie held up a newspaper, waiting for her daughter to come closer. "Nightclub owner gunned down in a brutal robbery," she read aloud. "It's a pity and a shame how they did your father."

"What?" she asked with a scrunched face.

"Juan Pablo, Kalie. He was your father."

"Wh... who?"

Queenie laid the old newspaper down on her desktop so that Kalie could take it and read it for herself. "He was my lover for many, many years," she explained. "It was supposed to be nothing more between us than our trades. He smuggled hungry girls from Cuba, and I put them on the street to give him a piece of the profits. Only the finest lay their heads under my roof. I knew that it would come out one day, and today just so happens to be that day."

"Why didn't I ever get to meet him?" Her eyes were still scanning the page. Particularly over the photo of the old Cuban man who looked so well-put together.

"Because it would've been shameful for a retired whore, turned madam, to show up at a married man's doorstep with a baby in her arms. You get my drift?"

"Did he even care about who I was? Did you ever tell him about me?"

"I did," she sadly confessed. "He thought it was best that we keep it strictly professional from that point on. I had to agree with him. Things had already gone too far."

Kalie slapped the newspaper back onto the desk with tears in her eyes and a hardened face.

"Don't you dare spill a tear over a man who didn't give a fuck enough to wish you a happy birthday."

"But you still accepted his whores?" she shouted.

"It was to keep you clothed, housed and fed, Kay!"

Kalie bit her lip to try and keep her tears at bay. "This is just one fucked up life, huh? You take what you're given, and you're not expected to feel a damn thing." She shrugged, throwing her hands up with a fake smile on her face. "Fine, mama. I won't feel shit. I'll accept that, too."

"Kalie, wait a second—"

"Forgive me for not being used to this life! If it's one thing that I know about you, it's that it's your way or no way, so you got that. But Kalie is living a life for Kalie. I regret that I never got to meet my father, but what the fuck can I do about it? Now you've planned my life thus far, but I've got it from here, *Mommy*."

"Kalie!"

There was nothing else to listen to. Kalie left the office and jogged up the stairs to her room. The first thing she did was drop down inside her computer chair to log onto her computer. She needed to check her bank account and open another online. That way, Queenie wouldn't be able to control anything else. She chose to only take out the money that she had earned from her clients, and transferred it over to the new account. Then, she placed a lock on her trust fund so that no one had the power to touch it. She would be giving that back to her mother so that she couldn't hold anything over her daughter's head.

Time seemed to have flown by— two hours to be exact— and Kalie had managed to contact six realty companies who had apartments in her price range. She would have to hold her sessions in her living room for the time being, until she earned enough to be able to lease a commercial space all by herself.

Her phone chimed on the corner of her desk. An alert let her know that her phone was finally down to five percent. She rolled her eyes at it and went over to her bed so that she could plug it up near her nightstand. Afterward, she opted to lay down in bed and cry. It was hard to believe that with a straight face, her mother would be willing to hide something so vital from her. But it was Queenie she was thinking about. Of course, it was possible.

A week had gone by. Scrappy hadn't heard from Kalie, but he figured that she was only busy with her practice. He, himself, had been extremely busy with work and going back and forth with Charles to prepare for his daughter's return.

Today was court day, and it was one hell of a day, at that. Scrappy sat reclined in his seat while the attorneys quietly argued at the bench. He just so happened to look over at Tamara with running mascara. She thought that presenting her lease and her expenses would help her out, but Charles kept to his word when making Scrappy look like a saint. The video that Scrappy took on the day of his wrongful arrest made matters worse for Tamara. Child Protective Services didn't take too kindly to it. Only a week without his daughter, as usual, was a breeze because he was anxiously awaiting her arrival home for good. To counter all of Tamara's claims of abuse and battery, Charles had character witnesses to take the stand and would also repeat how there were no previous police reports. Even Scrappy's text messages were printed for proof of his character, and to prove how verbally abusive Tamara was to him. His bank statements where he wired Tamara large amounts of money helped to bury her in her claim that he wasn't helping to support his child. Her allegations of him not properly taking care of Phara were shot to hell when Ms. Jackson and Stephanie took the stand to give their testimony of how often they see Tamara rather than Phara.

When the councilors were done, they retreated to their tables where they stood and waited for their clients to do so as well.

The old, white man on the bench looked at Tamara over the rim of his glasses with fiery rage in his eyes. "You, ma'am, are more than an unfit mother," he proclaimed with disdain. "You make all African American mothers spit upon your name, because you are a cliché that other cultures use in a punchline for racist jokes. Your house is a mess, your daughter is ten pounds underweight, there are no records of any checkups or up-to-date shots, you're unemployed, and you verbally abuse the only help that you have. With the way you spoke to him in these messages, and the way you bash him in these screen grabs from your social media, you should walk out of here with nothing. However, he is only obligated to pay your counter-claim for medical bills, which is a sum of $15,545 and no cents. You are responsible for your own court costs since you give foolish amounts for what you think he owes you. Tamara Dade, you are granted no custody of Phara Dade-Broadus—"

"What?" she shrieked.

"Compose yourself," the judge told her sternly. "Now, you are only granted two hours every Saturday for supervised visits."

"Your honor! This man beat my ass—"

He banged his gavel. "One more word and I'll have you in contempt! As I was saying." He then took his attention to Scrappy. "The next time you want to have a baby… make sure that it's with someone who is of sane mind and body, Mr. Broadus."

"Yes, your honor," Scrappy proudly answered.

"You still have to pay the remaining balance of your bail. As I see to it, by the power vested in me, through the state of Florida, you are now granted full custody of Phara Dade-Broadus, with no appeal unless agreed upon by you, sir. That's my ruling. It will stand as such." Once more, he banged his gavel to mark his decree.

Scrappy turned to Charles with a smile that exposed every last gold tooth in his skull, and exchanged a handshake that ended with him being caught inside a manly, celebratory hug.

"I told you, didn't I?" Charles gloated. "I told you that I would get your daughter back."

"Daddy!" Phara screamed.

Scrappy's head whirled around to see the lady that he was quite fond of now from Child Services standing beside an opened door. In a white dress and her hair in tight individual spiral curls, Phara took off running to her father, completely bypassing her mother, who was still in a raving fit about losing to Scrappy. He scooped her up in his arms and twirled with her. His lips were pressed against her cheek.

"Did you miss me?" he asked her.

Happily, Phara nodded with her hands on her father's cheeks.

Her beautiful orbs landed on a woman standing behind them, over the short wooden gate. "Who's she?" she innocently asked.

Scrappy turned to see Kalie standing there in a nice pair of slacks and a baby blue button up. "Well, Phara... this is, umm... This is daddy's friend. Her name is Kalie."

"Hello, Phara," Kalie greeted her with a smile.

"Bonjour."

"Aww, she speaks French."

"That's the bitch!" Tamara screamed from across the room.

The bailiffs were restraining her, but she wasn't a threat to Kalie. She stood there unmoved or undisturbed.

"That's the hoe you took my daughter from me over, you little spineless fucker? Fuck you, Scrappy! Oh, I'm gonna appeal so everybody can see what kind of man you really are!"

Kalie almost restored her smile when the officers were able to drag her out of the courtroom. Instead, she took her sights back to Phara.

"Congratulations," Ms. Jackson said to him as she approached, from down the aisle. "I see you got your life back."

Scrappy chuckled. "I got my baby back, too."

"I have to go because the shop ain't gonna run itself, but you stay up, child. Miss Phara, I'll be seeing you this weekend."

"Bye, Ms. Jackson," Phara said with a wave. "Daddy, can we go home?"

"Yes, baby," he agreed. "Can Kalie come, too?"

"Hmmm… yes."

Scrappy kissed her chubby cheek when she smiled, then locked fingers with Kalie's so that they could leave.

———————

When the group pulled into the driveway, there were cars parked along the street. The most noticeable were the tricked-out Mercury and the money green Lexus. Scrappy knew that his boys pulled one hell of a doozy just to celebrate his victory. There was no doubt in anyone's mind, except for Tamara's, that Scrappy wouldn't win his case. This was major to him. To hear and see on paper that Phara was all his was something to truly celebrate.

He got out of his car and pulled Phara over the rim of it since he rode with his top down. She liked it when there was no roof to the car. Afterward, he grabbed Kalie by the hand, who had already gotten out of her own car.

"Congratulations," she said. "How do you feel?"

"Oh, no. We're not doing that psych shit no more," he chuckled.

"So, what are we going to do about this? I mean, us?"

"What you think, college girl?"

"Scrappy, I'm moving out of my mama's house," she confessed.

Scrappy stopped and turned to her. "Well," he said with a smile. "I guess we'll have to start looking for places, then, huh?"

Kalie blushed. She loved his smile and she knew that it was because of Phara.

Scrappy opened the door to most of the people he knew, standing in his living room, screaming "Surprise!"

His smile grew with his daughter on his arm and his girl at his side. For now, Scrappy was on top of the world.

CHAPTER THIRTEEN

Payback's A Bitch In Heels

After cleaning up from the party, Scrappy stretched his tired muscles. Kalie came up behind him and wrapped her arms around his waist. He threw an arm around her and kissed her forehead. "How'd you sleep?" he asked her.

"You tell me, stallion," she responded with a giggle.

Scrappy looked behind her at how the dress shirt he wore the day before was sticking up at the height of her backside. "You look good in my shirt."

"You looked good inside me last night."

"Ooh, you so nasty."

"I still have the footage on my phone."

"You recorded us?"

"Why not?" Kalie twirled around to position herself in front of him with her arms still around his waist. "You're going to be busy working and so will I. We'll only get to see each other on the weekends, possibly, so I needed a keepsake."

"Ahh, okay. So there's a reason to your insanity."

"There is."

"Aside from the freaky shit, how did you enjoy your night?"

Kalie leaned her head back to let her curls fall. It gave Scrappy the perfect view of her bosom peeking from behind the fabric of his shirt. "Oh my God, Scrap... Phara is so wonderful. She's intelligent, and she even taught me a little French. Well, that's only because I had to catch on to what she was saying because she mixes her French with her English."

"Like most Haitians."

"She was so bright... like... that's the only way that I could describe it. And Ms. Jackson? She thought that my hair was a well-done weave."

Scrappy had to chuckle at that one.

"She had to put her fingers at my scalp, just to make sure that I wasn't lying to her. Oh, and, what does '*li bezwen manje*' mean?"

Scrappy laughed again, throwing his head back.

"What? Tell me," she pouted.

"It means that you need to eat."

Kalie gasped. "So, what is '*mens ti fi*'? She kept calling me that all night."

"Oh my God. Did you answer to that?"

"I did. Why?"

"Kay," he laughed. "She was calling you 'skinny girl.'"

Kalie sucked her teeth and walked away from him.

He gently caught her by her wrist to pull her so that her back was resting against his front. "It's cool, baby," he whispered in her ear. "Ain't nothin' wrong with your figure. I love it."

"Thank you, Scrappy," she grinned. "I had fun, but it's back to work I go."

"Oh man, come on, boo. You gon' leave me like this?"

"I don't want to, but this apartment isn't going to finance itself. Other than that, you have to spend some time with Phara before she goes to see her mama later."

"Why'd you book this appointment on a Saturday, anyway?"

"Extra income," she laughed.

"Will you come back?"

"Of course I will. I won't be a minute later than eight."

"Why so long?"

"Because, Scrap... This client is only artistically expressive. He's an OCD client, so he had to book even numbers. Besides, it'll give you some time to miss me."

He wrapped his arms tighter around her waist. He wasn't used to feeling so vulnerable, but he loved it a little too much to let a good thing like Kalie go for now.

"Oh, he's paying almost a grand for this one session," she added. "I won't be that far away from you. I'll be at the Hilton downtown. So, as soon as I finish up there, I promise I will be on my way back. You can have me through Sunday night."

Scrappy kissed her shoulder, accepting her promise. It wasn't easy to gain trust from someone like him, but something in him said he could trust Kalie.

———————

Angrily, Mocha stormed into Dolla's home, ready to give him yet another earful. What was in her hand was something that would make him pass out. He already knew that she was there by the loud clack of her heels against his marble floor. He stood from the pool table where he was enjoying someone else's mouth for a change. This time, he decided not to hide the fact that she wasn't the only one anymore.

As soon as Mocha turned the corner, she stopped dead in her tracks. The girl on her knees rose to her feet and looked between the two.

"So, you don't have me out here lookin' stupid?" Mocha asked Dolla. "Then who the fuck is this bitch?"

"Hoe, get out," Dolla told the young girl as he stuffed his dick back inside his briefs.

Mocha eyed the girl as she passed, then threw the pregnancy test that she had at him. "Fuck you and all this shit, Dolla!" she spat.

He rubbed his hands together with his head tilted. "I told you about that mouth, didn't I?"

"You heard what the fuck I said, nigga. I spent all these fuckin' years bringin' you information about my mama's moves, and this is what you do to me? You play me out?"

"You played yourself, girl. You ain't been useful to me in years."

"Useful?" she scoffed. "You know what? I'm done with you. For good. Don't worry about this baby either. I'm gettin' an abortion." Mocha spun around on the balls of her feet while mumbling under her breath. She was almost at the door when a large hand grabbed her shoulder.

She ended up being dragged up steps by the back of her neck. It didn't matter how hard she fought or how badly she scratched Dolla up, he wasn't letting her go. He flung her inside his bedroom and shut the door behind him.

"So, fuck me, huh?" he taunted her. "You do that."

"No!" she shouted with mascara running down her face.

"Mocha, get your ass over here and work me off. *Now!*"

"I said no!"

"Okay." Dolla nodded as he approached her. "You'll regret this shit, bitch. You, your mama, and your uppity ass sisters. Now, get the fuck out of my house." Dolla left her sitting on the floor, stopping at the door to turn around to her. "Oh, and if you kill off my seed... I'm gonna fuckin' kill you."

Mocha sat there shivering. She brought this upon herself. All she had to do was keep watch over him, but she ended up falling in love with someone who was clearly not for her. No matter how much she didn't want to believe the only thing she had to do, it was evident that she had to go home to her mother and ask for help. Dolla couldn't get away with treating her like shit.

She thought he loved her. She also thought that being with him would get her away from Queenie's controlling ways. Sitting there, reevaluating it all, Queenie was the only way out of this sticky situation.

Mocha rose to her feet and went down the stairs where she found Dolla speaking to the young girl just outside of the doors. He was most likely trying to convince her to stay a while just to finish the job since Mocha wasn't going to do it. In true Mocha fashion, she sucked up her tears, how her mother taught her, strutted through the foyer and over the threshold, then pulled her fist back to seven years ago before Dolla wooed her into his clutches. With her fist flying, in that tiny window, she knew what was coming after she assaulted him. Being the daughter of a queen, which was who she forgot she was, granted her access of paradise. Not the hell that Dolla put her in.

As soon as Dolla turned to her with a cocked brow, Mocha's fist slammed into the side of his face. She had done something no man was able to do with their bare hands, which was knock him to the floor. Then, Mocha spat on him and took off running to her waiting Mercedes.

"Fuck you, Dolla!" she screamed once inside. "I said we're done! And I'm telling my Mommy, motherfucker!"

Dolla picked himself up off the concrete with his throbbing jaw in his hand, and fiery eyes at the speeding Mercedes. Mocha would have to pay for that.

―――――――――

Kalie had wrapped up with her client, gave him a few encouraging words, then booked him to see her the following Saturday afternoon. She was so sure that this one man was going to get her inside a house that she was going to section off for her clients. With a smile, she led him to the door. He pulled down the L-shaped handle four different times before he finally exited.

As soon as he stepped out, the door was being pushed back open. She could've sworn that it was her client, but it wasn't. She turned around when reaching her notepad to look back at him. Her jaw fell flat onto the carpet.

"Hey, baby," Bandz said. "Do you know how long I stood out there, waiting for you to finish up?"

Kalie eyed him strangely. "Why are you here?" she asked lowly.

"I needed to see you."

"And? How did you know that I was here?"

"I went to see Scrap earlier, only to see you comin' out of his place. Oh, and I saw the kiss that you gave him, too."

Kalie gulped. She backed away until she fell into the chair that client had just gotten out of. The low tone in his voice and his bloodshot eyes made her fear him.

"That's why you've been avoiding me? Because of him? Because what? He came between us, Kalie, and you let him."

She slowly shook her head.

"You did. But why? Was I not good enough for you? Was I not savage enough?"

"Bandz," she merely said, no higher than that of a whisper. "You fucked up your first chance by nutting too early. Then, you almost killed me. Lastly, you fucked someone else after you gave me those sappy messages. What makes you think that you deserve another chance with me? You blew them all."

"You don't get it, Kalie. I need you. You have become a piece of me—"

"You were with someone else, Bandz."

"She was nothing to me."

"But you still did it."

"Mocha wasn't shit to me, alright? It's you that I want."

Kalie's face contorted. Her head tilted. "What?"

"You heard me. I want you, not her."

"You fucked my sister?"

"You're missing my point—"

Somehow, Kalie found the courage to stand and point to the door. "Leave, now."

"Baby—"

"Go! I can't even believe you right now!"

"Is it because you want that crazy ass motherfucker, Scrap?"

"You're more crazy than he is to even stand here to admit that you fucked my sister!"

Bandz took three steps over to her, only leaving six inches between them. "What is it going to take for you to respect me, girl? I'm motherfuckin' Bandz. I get bitches badder than you any time."

"Then go get them!"

Without warning, Bandz backhanded Kalie over onto the coffee table. He was about to apologize for what he had done until he saw the terror in her eyes. She was beneath him. That's how he wanted it to be. He had finally broken precious Baby K.

Roughly, he grabbed her by the collar and dragged her into the master bedroom where he tossed her onto the bed.

Her screams only aroused him. "Fuck that," he said through closed teeth while trying to hold her wrists down on the made bed. "You just had to be fuckin' difficult."

Kalie used her flexibility to bring her leg around his waist to push him off with her foot. Bandz was too strong for her. He pulled her down onto the floor, but twisted to where he would land on top.

"You *will* respect me," he promised her.

Kalie head-butted him to try and get him off, but ended up doing more damage to herself. Bandz ripped her top open. He didn't feel a thing when she scratched him across the face. Instead of getting off of her, he lifted her skirt and ripped open her panties with both her wrist now being held down by only one of his hands.

"Get off!" she screamed.

"I'm gonna give you somethin' to remember me by, Kay. You're gonna be with me whether you like it or not."

CHAPTER FOURTEEN

Goodnight, Sweet Royals

Scrappy knocked on the door of Tamara's with his dreads pulled behind his back and his attire well-put together. Kalie would be coming by the house in a few, so he was going to have to make his pickup quickly, and get back so that he could get Phara settled and ready for bed.

Tamara opened the door with tears in her eyes. Meekly, she backed up to let him in.

"Thousand feet," he mumbled, referring to the restraining order that he had against her. It was only void in that moment had it had something to do with his daughter. The supervisor from child services would always be a witness to that.

Instead of running to him, Phara walked over from the couch and hugged his leg. She was still clean and still smelled good from when he dropped her off. Surprisingly, Tamara's living room was spotless. There was still a hint of the scent of weed in the air, but it wasn't his place to judge. The supervisor would be taking notes of that. To Scrappy, Tamara was digging her own grave.

"Mr. Broadus, may I have a word?" the middle-aged white woman asked him. She stood from the couch and tucked her clipboard under her arm.

Scrappy obliged as he picked Phara up off the floor. She buried her head inside her father's chest. He could feel her heart rapidly beating.

The woman cleared her throat as Tamara slipped out the front door for a moment. "She was running around the backyard just a few minutes ago. I saw in her file that she was an asthmatic, but Ms. Dade informed me that it was only for a little while and that Phara would've been okay. Is she correct?"

Scrappy rubbed Phara's back as Tamara re-entered with her hands tucked inside her armpits. "No, she's not," he admitted. "I'll keep a closer eye on her to see how she's breathing. Thank you, Miss."

"No problem, Mr. Broadus."

Scrappy bid the supervisor who watched over Phara and Tamara a good night. He was almost at his car when Tamara ran out onto the lawn to grab his attention. "Scrappy!" she called him. "I love you!"

"Tamara, you got a thousand-foot rule," he told her while helping his daughter into the car over the door. "You need to abide by that and get the fuck on with the bullshit."

"I don't want to do this until she's eighteen! Just... please—"

"Man, you won't have to do it until she's eighteen. She'll be able to make her own decisions when she's *thirteen*."

"Scrappy, I love you!" she blurted.

He looked back at her after opening his car door with a smirk on.

Tamara stood there in her long, brown garden dress, looking like nothing to him.

He shook his head and got into his car without so much as a response.

With a smile, he drove to his home, holding pleasant conversation with his daughter. There was something oddly different in her tone. As he pulled into the driveway, he narrowed his lids at her.

"Phara, you okay?" he asked worriedly.

She nodded with a frown.

He knew that she was only trying to be a big girl, so he decided to keep a closer eye on her.

Scrappy took his daughter out her booster seat and traveled into the house with her backpack strapped over one of his shoulders. With her propped on his arm, he could hear the rattle in her chest. He kissed her cheek and sat her on the couch.

"Does your chest hurt?" he asked her.

She lightly nodded as she caressed the large red heart on her t-shirt.

Scrappy threw the backpack onto the coffee table, unzipped it, and quickly rummaged through to find her inhaler. Past her dolls and snacks that she didn't get a chance to eat, there was no inhaler in sight. Then, he rushed into the kitchen to go through the drawers in case he had stored the emergency inhaler there. There was nothing. Scrappy went back to his daughter to have her put her hands on top of her head to try and get her to open her airways so that she could breathe.

"Inhale and exhale slowly, Phara," he instructed her in a very tender voice.

Out of the door he blazed to get to the car and so that he could go through his glove compartment to find the inhaler that he stored there. He had always kept one there since she was a year old. He remembered telling Tamara that she was going to have to keep one in her glovebox as well so that they could prevent attacks in the future.

Then, in the middle of pulling out napkins, parking tickets that he already paid, and random receipts, he remembered the supervisor telling him about Phara's visit, when Tamara slipped out of the front door. There was no reason for her to leave the house, unless…

Scrappy slammed the glove box and bolted back into the house. Phara lay on the floor in front of the couch with her eyes on nothing in particular. He rushed over to her and sat on the floor to pull her up to his lap. Gently, he placed her in a full-nelson while coaching her to breathe. He had to fight with himself to pull his cellphone out of his pocket with a shaky hand just to dial 9-1-1.

"Nine-one-one, what's your emergency?"

"Edwin Broadus… My daughter's having an asthma attack—"

"Does she have albuterol near, sir?"

"No." His voice was shaking. "Her arms are above her head to try and get her to breathe."

"What's the address?"

"136 Northeast 150th Street."

"Sir, do you know CPR?"

"Yes." His voice had become hardly inaudible, just underneath the sounds of Phara's light wheezing.

"How old is your daughter?"

"Three."

"If she stops breathing before help arrives, you must perform CPR. Help is on the way."

Scrappy hung up and threw his phone over his shoulder onto the couch. He held Phara's chest with one hand as he rocked with her. Then, it hit him that he had honey in the kitchen. He stood with Phara in his arms and briskly walked into the kitchen to the cupboard, where he pulled down the jar of honey. With an easy pop of the lid, he held the jar up to her nose. "Breathe it in, baby. Open your mouth and inhale it, as much as you can."

Phara tried, but her breaths were very short.

"Come on, baby. Breathe for Daddy."

She inhaled though all you could hear was her wheezing. They had become more and more silent with every breath she had taken, yet Scrappy only thought that the honey trick was working. That was until Phara's arms fell limply over his.

In a hurry, he gently laid her on the table and placed a loaf of bread underneath her neck so that her head would recline. With tears in his eyes, he leaned down to check to hear if she was breathing. He couldn't hear a thing. He slid the jar of honey across the table and started to press his hands into her chest. With every pump, he hoped and prayed that he would be able to save her the same way he saved Kalie. Afterward, he blew into her little lungs twice, trying to get her to breathe.

"Come on, baby," he said with a chopping voice as he pressed her chest some more. "Breathe for Daddy. Breathe, Phara. Breathe, baby. Come on."

Being that he lived in Little Haiti, he knew that the ambulance wasn't going to arrive in time to save the only priceless possession that he had.

However, cherry and blue lights appeared through the curtains of his dining room window. Still, he tried all he could, yet Phara's lips were already turning blue. Her little hands flopped with every push to her chest, and Scrappy's heart was shattering.

A heavy knock came to his door. "Paramedics!"

He couldn't return a statement. He, instead, gave his daughter powerful gusts to get her to at least cough.

The first responders entered on their own and found him still trying CPR on his daughter. One short and stocky white man moved him aside and fit a mask over Phara's face. Scrappy took a few steps back as he crumbled inside. Tears were wetting his cheeks while the other responder was asking him questions. He couldn't answer them. He was deaf to all of the words that were coming to him.

"How long have you been performing CPR, sir?" the man asked louder.

"About… about five minutes," he muttered.

"We need to get her on the rig, *now!*" Easily, the man scooped Phara off the table and laid her on a stretcher while the other pumped a bag attached to the mask.

It didn't look like she would be breathing anytime soon.

The man holding the bag placed his ear at her chest. "Her heart isn't beating. We need the defibrillator."

"Sir, come with us."

Without his phone and locking up the house, Scrappy followed the stretcher into the back of the ambulance, where they had no choice but to cut open Phara's shirt to place stickers onto her chest and ribs. Then came the clamps to the wires of the heart monitor. Scrappy didn't take his eyes off of his little princess. They gave her two shocks to the chest, yet each time didn't conjure a result.

With each flatline, Scrappy was losing his own breath.

With his digits wrapped around Kalie's throat, Bandz gave her three last pumps. After the last, he let out a wall-shaking growl as his knees buckled. Kalie could barely breathe by the time Bandz pulled out of her. She was numb from shock and had absentmindedly gone into some other place in her mind. She had three broken nails from how hard she fought to get him off of her, and a bruised cheek and forehead from how hard he fought her back. Her lips were split, she had a chipped tooth, and there were scratches on the insides of her thighs. There was no doubt in her mind that he would pay for what he had done to her. She literally had a body of proof.

"Fuck," Bandz grunted. His orgasm was too strong for him to stand up right away. He came three times, back to back, splashing all of his semen inside of her each time. "You do got golden pussy," he said with a raspy voice. "My brother was right."

Finally, he stood up and stuffed his dick back inside his briefs and jeans.

"I did that because I love you," he told her with pride. "This is what happens when you disobey, or when you give my shit away. You stay the fuck away from Scrappy, or else it will be a lot worse next time. I just might fuck around and kill you. You belong to me. You understand?"

Kalie's eyes were on the foot of the bed at her left; she had been lying on the floor for the past forty-five minutes.

When she didn't answer, Bandz kicked her in the ribs. "Bitch, I said do you understand me!"

Still, she couldn't answer, though she writhed in pain. All she could do was lay there and cry.

"You better understand that. And if you tell anybody that I raped you instead of made love to you… that bitch mother and whore sisters of yours will meet an end. I'm Bandz, baby. I can make it happen. Either you're mine, or you'll suffer."

Kalie didn't watch him walk away. She laid there in her own blood and juices, quietly sobbing. After the front door clasped shut, it made her flinch. She cried more, all until the volume of her sobs stopped completely. Her face drew blank. She remembered that mentally, she was too strong for a fucking idiot like Bandz. There would be too many people around her to protect her in the event that he tried something stupid.

Weakly, Kalie crawled into the living room of the suite, past the coffee table to get to her phone on the chair where she was sitting with her client almost an hour prior. She found Scrappy's contact and clicked on it to tell him what had just happened. When she got his voicemail, her face scrunched as more tears poured out of her eyes. Then, she found Sheena's contact.

"My little sissy!" Sheena sang happily after the first ring.

"Hey sister-in-law!" Legend cheerily greeted her in the background.

"Shut up!" Sheena giggled. "Baby K, what's up?"

Kalie tried to get her words in order, but nothing would come out of her mouth.

"Kalie!"

"What's the matter?" Legend asked.

Kalie took a deep breath. "I'm at the Hilton downtown," she said as calmly as possible. "Someone raped me."

"I'm on my way."

"Baby!" Legend screamed. "I need to get to Scrap!"

"Hold on, Kay." Sheena pulled the phone away from her ear. "What's wrong?"

"I don't know. Calmly texted me and said get there. You want me to drop you at Kay on my way?"

"Do that. Kalie, I'm on my way!"

The line went dead and Kalie felt like dying. *What could've happened to Scrappy?* she thought. It was too much for her, though; all she could do was rest her back against the chair. She was going to have to suck up her pride and get down to the lobby, looking the mess she was and face her sister to tell her what happened. Bandz was a dead man after killing her inside.

Whether she liked it or not, she was yet another pawn between the king and queen of Miami. She was a spoil of a war that had yet to spark. Her mother would paint the streets with the blood of her enemy for what had just happened to her baby.

TO BE CONTINUED

ACKNOWLEDGEMENTS

I have a very long list of incredible readers, yet I don't have the capacity to single you out, because I might forget someone and they might wind up mad at me over it. So, THANK YOU ALL FOR THE CONTINUED SUPPORT AND LOVE! You know you're the best. Your numbers seem to grow with each and every release, and you make me one happy author!

Porscha Sterling and Quiana Nicole, you are two hard working women that I'm lucky to work with… when I'm not pestering you for no reason at all. With each release, no matter the bumps in the road, if there are any, you two ladies smooth it out and get it done with ease. What can I say? I guess that's just what royals do.

Rooooob! Robin Conner, you have become one of my Ace Boons, and I have to say that checking my inbox every day for the last few months has been an adventure. If any normal person were to hack our accounts and tried to keep up without conversations, they would truly end up lost and scratching their heads. Thank you for being a vociferous weirdo like me. I'm not alone! Keep droppin' heat like you've been doing. I'm proud of you!

Keish Andrea and Jaimme Jaye, y'all are the truth. What I learned from you is to never judge a book by its cover, and that's only because y'all look innocent, but you keep me laughing until I'm crying. You two are amazing young women in your prime. I can see you soaring further and wallowing in your continued success. Salute!

Larissa, Misty, both Jasmines, Kendra Rainey and Shavekia, you are my A-1's. I love your honesty and your humor. Without you gals, I might have a limp in my step. Remain the goddesses you are and continue to prosper through all of the hardships and rainy days. I love you!

My family and distant friends, I love you. There's no disputing that. I keep you all close for a reason. That's why I praise you when I can or give you comfort. Thank you so much for all that you've done for me. You are appreciated.

Sunny Giovanni

OTHER ROYAL RELEASES
FROM SUNNY

Chosen: A Street King's Obsession (1 -3)

Givana & Slay: A No Questions Asked Love Story

A Forbidden Street King's Love Story

A Forbidden Street King's Love Story 2:
Through Hell & High Water

Love & Cocaine: A Savage Love Story

Love & Cocaine 2: For Better or Worse

Stuck on You: Shane & Cherie's Story (1 - 4)

Obsessed with a Savage

Caught Between Two Street Kings

CONNECT WITH SUNNY!

Twitter & Instagram: @imthatgiovanni

Tumblr: knojokegio.tumblr.com

Google Plus: Sunny Giovanni

Facebook: https://www.facebook.com/thesunnygiovanni/

Looking for a publishing home?

Royalty Publishing House, Where the Royals reside, is accepting submissions for writers in the urban fiction genre. If you're interested, submit the first 3-4 chapters with your synopsis to submissions@royaltypublishinghouse.com.

Check out our website for more information: www.royaltypublishinghouse.com.

Text ROYALTY to 42828 to join our mailing list!

To submit a manuscript for our review, email us at submissions@royaltypublishinghouse.com

Text RPHCHRISTIAN to 22828 for our CHRISTIAN ROMANCE novels!

Text RPHROMANCE to 22828 for our INTERRACIAL ROMANCE novels!

Get LiT!

Download the LiTeReader app today and enjoy exclusive content, free books, and more

Do You Like CELEBRITY GOSSIP?

Check Out QUEEN DYNASTY!
Visit Our Site: www.thequeendynasty.com

CPSIA information can be obtained
at www.ICGtesting.com
Printed in the USA
LVOW13s0044240617

539175LV00018B/396/P